For the Royal Brompton Hospital – a place that has saved me so many times.

The Football Superstar

The Charlie Fry Series

Part Five

Martin Smith

1. STINKER

Rexy stank.

He reached to grab his ancient phone from the bedside cabinet and his own stench nearly made him sick.

He could not remember the last time he'd had a shower.

Yesterday? No.

Had he even washed this week?

Rexy couldn't remember. He did not care: he had been too busy celebrating to wash.

He looked at his phone: 11.36am.

It was time to get up.

He swung his legs over the side of the bed, as the springs groaned under his weight, and stood up.

He rubbed his eyes on the way to the toilet and managed to step in the remains of last night's Chinese takeaway.

It didn't matter. There was no chance he would clean up. He would soon leave – he never stayed anywhere long.

No-one ever visited so, as long as he didn't mind

the mess, what was the problem?

Rexy didn't have a job.

He didn't need to.

He was a crook – and a clever one.

The police had never caught him and he intended to keep it that way.

He may be a pig at home but, in public, his appearance transformed.

Rexy washed, combed his hair and wore fresh clothes.

His dark hair was kept short and his beard stubble was immaculate.

Aged in his mid-thirties, Rexy was not tall and had a ring of flab around the tummy. He was normal – the perfect disguise. He blended in and no-one took notice of him.

His mobile phone rang as Rexy finished his wee.

He did not wash his hands or flush the loo.

The words 'Private Number' flashed in front of him.

Rexy shrugged. People often did not want to leave a record. He was used to dealing with mysterious private numbers.

"Yes?

"Ah, hello Mr Di Santos, it has been a long time."

He kept the phone pressed to his ear and raised an eyebrow with surprise.

"It is short notice but it can be done. Of course, a tight deadline means it will cost more."

Rexy listened again.

Finally he replied.

"That sounds fine. Who is the target?"

Rexy's eyes widened with shock.

He spluttered: "Are you being serious? He is

probably the most famous person in this town!

"This is a hell of a risky job and will cost a lot more than usual. My services don't come cheap but this is something else."

He could feel his neck get hotter.

Rexy puffed out his cheeks. "I'm glad money does not matter – because this is going to be seriously expensive."

He nodded a final time.

"Okay, as long as we are clear: I will get the job done and then I'll be leaving the country.

"Send over the first half of the money today and you've got a deal.

"We'll never work together again after this because it is too risky."

He hung up without waiting for a response.

Chell Di Santos was a crazy man. But he paid well.

Charlie Fry was the most famous person in Crickledon at the moment.

Now Rexy had to stop the Football Boy Wonder from playing in next weekend's championship decider.

2. PLOT

Chell Di Santos ended the call.

He allowed the briefest of smiles and leaned back into the expensive office chair to consider his options.

Six days until the game that would define his destiny.

If he won, he would get his chance in the Football League. Perhaps even the Premier League.

After all, he would be the football manager who took on the so-called Football Boy Wonder and won.

If he lost, he....

No, he would not consider that.

It would not happen. He only needed a point. If Rovers avoided defeat, they would be champions.

They just had to stop Charlie Fry.

Di Santos straightened the black sleeves of his designer shirt, stretched and placed both hands behind his head.

Nothing would get in the way of his beautiful career in management.

He was going to have it all. Money. Fame. A place

in history.

Nobody would stop him.

It certainly would not be Charlie Fry and his gang of wannabe football stars.

The boy opposite him coughed and shuffled in his seat.

Di Santos had forgotten Adam Knight was there.

He spoke quickly.

"It is done.

"The so-called Boy Wonder will play no part in Saturday's match.

"You have played your part to perfection."

Eyes shining brightly, Di Santos smiled wickedly.

The thought of Charlie Fry being unable to stop him was a wonderful one.

"Now I will keep my end of the bargain.

"Your spying on Charlie Fry was excellent. He is a cheat.

"Whatever magic power he has, it cannot be legal. He does not deserve to play football ever again. I will ensure his career is finished."

Adam grinned at the thought of Charlie's football career being ruined.

"How?"

Di Santos continued: "Do not worry about the details.

"It is a tricky situation, particularly as we have no concrete evidence."

Adam moved uneasily in his seat.

He began: "I tried…."

Di Santos silenced him with a wave of the hand.

"It matters not. We may not know every detail.

"The fact is we know he is cheating.

"Now, we do not have the required proof to go to

the authorities … but there are other ways around this problem."

Di Santos's eyes lit up. His smile widened as Adam shifted in his seat, unable to hide his own nerves.

"Our little friend won't be playing on Saturday. I have made sure of that.

"As a result, Rovers will be champions. And next year, we will go on to even greater things."

Di Santos paused for a second and then added dramatically: "You will be my striker and captain in the future."

Adam grinned and cracked his knuckles loudly in celebration.

Di Santos forced the smile to remain on his face – despite a small shudder at the revolting sound.

He detested the slimy kid sitting in front of him.

Adam though did not seem to notice.

"Excellent. Colts have kicked me out, I dunno why.

"They said they were unhappy with my attitude or something pathetic like that.

"They are such losers. I'll be banging in goals for you left, right and centre."

Adam had been top scorer in the league until last week when Magpies – inspired by Charlie – had scored in the last minute to knock Thrapborough Colts out of the title race.

Secretly Chell Di Santos did not care. He would not be managing Hall Park Rovers next year so his promises meant nothing.

Adam Knight would be someone else's problem.

Bigger things awaited the 'Spanish Supremo' – as the Crickledon Telegraph had begun calling him.

Still he needed to pretend for a few more days.

The young fool had helped him to discover Charlie Fry's cheating – even if neither of them knew exactly how the strange target worked.

Di Santos continued: "Sometimes a club and a player are a natural fit.

"Brian Bishop's attitude has never been good enough so he will not play for my team again. You will be the main man."

Adam pushed the chair back on to two legs.

"Hell yeah, boss! Next year will be our year."

Neither of them noticed the crouched shadow that lurked outside the office as they spoke.

Slowly the boy inched away from the window.

Then he turned and ran.

Within seconds, Brian Bishop was away and pulled out his mobile phone.

The Rovers striker knew what to do.

He had a friend to save.

3. WAITING

Crickledon Rec was popular at weekends.

Children loved the huge climbing frames and the oceans of neatly cut grass made it ideal for a picnic on a warm day.

But by early Sunday evening most of the families had headed home – in preparation for the school week ahead.

Apart from a few dog walkers on the other side of the park, the Rec was quiet.

It was the perfect place for Charlie Fry and his friends to meet so they were not overhead.

Charlie kicked the ball against a tree.

His mates Joe Foster and Peter Bell were perched on a wooden bench nearby but Charlie could not sit for another second.

Normally, he would try not to show his friends that he was nervous. Or excited. Or anxious.

But today was different.

The Football Boy Wonder had been worried ever since Joe had rung earlier saying to meet down the

Rec.

His friend sounded different.

Charlie raced to their usual meeting spot – and found Joe and Peter already there.

Tension filled the air. There was none of the usual banter between the friends – the high-fives and mickey-taking was missing.

Joe did not have much more to add. He simply said Bishop had insisted they needed to hear something – and had not given any further clues.

Unable to sit any longer, Charlie had grabbed the football and booted it around their usual makeshift pitch.

Peter piped up first: "Chell Di Santos is behind this. I know it."

Charlie shrugged and pushed a hand through his short blonde hair.

Peter was probably right: the Hall Park Rovers manager had never liked him and had been delighted to kick him out of the Rovers set-up.

But Charlie had proved him wrong.

He was now the leading scorer in the Crickledon Under-13s league as Hall Park Magpies – who gave him the chance to save his football career – surged up the league.

Everything had changed: everyone knew his name; people wanted his autograph; a group of girls followed him home from school, much to Charlie's embarrassment.

Best of all, Premier League scouts wanted to sign him. It was like a dream.

Peter and Joe moved towards Charlie so they could not be overheard.

"It is obvious, isn't it? He is obsessed with you,

Fry.

"He is a crazy man. Who spies on an 11-year-old? He is barmy – a power-crazed fool."

Charlie smiled. The thought was ludicrous: had Di Santos really convinced Adam Knight to spy on him? It was insane.

"Yeah I know. I just ... sometimes wish this had never happened to me."

Peter put hands on both of Charlie's shoulders.

"Look at me, dipstick.

"Never, ever think that again."

Charlie pulled a face and tried to pull away but Peter forced him to remain looking in his direction.

"I mean it, Fry-inho.

"You didn't ask for the lightning bolt to nearly kill you.

'Nor did you ask for it to stick a magic target in your head ... and turn you into the world's greatest footballer!"

Charlie's lip twitched. He struggled to find the right words.

"It is ... just ... am I cheating? Should I be allowed to use the target in my head?

"Am I really a great footballer or is it the target?

"What happens if Di Santos tells everyone ... and they believe him?"

Charlie's cheeks began to burn as he blurted out the words.

Since they discovered Adam Knight had been spying, his mind had been filled with doubts.

Joe jumped in before Peter could reply.

"Cut it out, Charlie.

"No-one makes an exception for you on the football field because you have cystic fibrosis, do they?"

Charlie paused for a second to think.

Joe continued without an answer: "No, they don't. No-one lets you score because you can't breathe.

"No-one runs slower towards the ball because you don't have much puff, do they?"

Charlie could see what Joe was getting at.

Joe added: "Of course they don't! Sport is about being competitive!

"So why should you be singled out for using something inside your mind?

"It is part of you whether you want it or not. It is none of their business.

"Besides when you got hit by the lightning bolt, the hospital ran all sorts of tests and said you were fine. Didn't they?"

Charlie thought back to his hospital stay after the accident. It seemed such a long time ago.

"Yeah, you're right...."

Joe punched him playfully on the arm.

"Of course, I'm right. The magic target is part of you. It is not cheating or the hospital would have tried to remove it.

"Instead, they couldn't even find it. Whether you like it or not, the target is here to stay."

For the first time in days, Charlie smiled. The magic target floated harmlessly in his vision as usual.

"I guess so. Thanks guys."

A voice interrupted the boys.

"Where is everyone?"

Bishop looked like he was going to be sick. He bent forward to get air into his lungs.

"I brought Charlie and Peter. Who else did you want?" asked Joe.

Bishop took a moment to catch his breath.

Finally he straightened up, filled his lungs with air and spoke with determination.

"I meant bring everyone, all of Magpies. We are going to need everyone.

"It is happening. They are coming for Charlie."

4. ALL FOR ONE

Twenty minutes later, half the Magpies team stood between the trees that acted as goalposts during regular kickabouts.

Annie Cooper, Darren 'Mudder' Bunnell, Toby Grace, Emma Tysoe, Gary Bradshaw and Billy Savage were standing waiting.

Joe spoke up: "Right Bishop. We're all here. What's this big news?"

Bishop had barely spoken since his arrival.

It was so unusual. He may have been the star striker for Chell Di Santos's team but he was still their friend.

Like Joe, he put friendship before football.

But today he was acting strangely.

"Is this everyone?" Charlie noticed Bishop's eyes flick towards the gates as if he was anxious about being overheard.

Joe shrugged. "Flem was getting his haircut. Wrecka, Jimmy, Theo and Greavesy didn't answer their phones.

"We can fill them in on the details – once we know what we are dealing with."

Bishop beckoned everyone to step closer towards him.

When the group surrounded him, he spoke in a whisper so no-one could overhear the conversation.

"Charlie is in danger.

"Chell Di Santos has hatched some sort of plan to stop him playing in the derby next week."

Charlie's Hall Park Magpies would face sister club Hall Park Rovers next weekend. The winning team would win the Crickledon Under-13s title.

Peter pounded a fist into his palm. "I knew it! What is he planning?"

Bishop shrugged.

"I don't know. I overheard him telling Adam Knight."

There were several gasps.

Joe spoke through gritted teeth. "Adam Knight?"

Bishop nodded, unable to keep the look of disgust off his face.

"I know. Worse still, he is here to stay. He's going to be a Rovers player next season."

The group stood silent as they absorbed the news. The bully was hardly the most popular person among the Magpies players.

Joe sighed. "I guess that was predictable. What else did he say?"

Bishop shook his head: "I didn't hear much. Di Santos said he had taken care of matters and Charlie would not be playing on Saturday."

Bishop looked towards Charlie. "And he kept calling you a cheat."

Charlie blushed and looked at the floor. Bishop

did not know about the magic target, despite being a mate.

Only Peter, Joe and Annie had been trusted with his secret. Now Toby knew as well after they had mistaken him for the football spy last week.

The others didn't know.

Charlie could see the confusion on their faces as they tried to understand why Di Santos would make the claim.

Annie responded first. "Why should we trust you? You are one of his favourites, aren't you?"

Charlie tried not to laugh. Typical Annie, he thought. She would defend him against anyone.

She did not know Bishop like the others – and she always put Charlie first.

Bishop threw his hands in the air at the questions.

Charlie piped up: "No, Annie. We can trust him.

"Bishop is a good guy – he is one of us. He likes Di Santos about as much as Peter does."

The group laughed. Annie, though, was not fully convinced.

"How did you hear this? Surely they weren't wandering the streets so anybody could overhear them?"

Mudder spoke for the first time. "Yeah, Annie's right. What were you doing there?"

It was Bishop's turn to become embarrassed. "I … overheard them. I…."

Joe patted his shoulder. "Just say how it is, Bish."

No-one argued. Bishop took a deep breath and spoke slowly.

"I heard the rumours. I knew my place was in danger despite the goals.

"Adam Knight has been telling everyone that he

would be the Rovers striker in the future.

"If that happens, where does that leave me? I'll be on the bench at best.

"So I went to front up Di Santos – and find out where I stood. But, as I approached his office, the window was open and I heard my name so I stopped…."

Bishop's voice tailed off.

"What happened then?"

Bishop continued: "They were in there: Di Santos and Knight. The best buddies were having a cosy chat.

"I couldn't hear everything but I did hear him say that Adam Knight would be the Rovers striker – and he would take my place.

"I'm finished at Rovers. Then I heard his plot against you – so I turned and ran. I knew you needed to know as soon as possible."

Charlie looked at Bishop with admiration. His Rovers career had gone up in smoke – yet his first instinct was to help others.

Not many people would do that.

Bishop stood up to his full height. He was tall. In the group in front of him, only Joe came near him.

"Now I want to help.

"Charlie must play next week and his friends – no matter what team they play for – need to make sure that happens."

Peter slapped Bishop on the shoulder. "Well said. Now what's the plan?"

5. TEAMWORK

The plan was simple.

They never left Charlie alone.

When he was walking to school, during break and walking home – there was always at least two of the gang with him.

The friends discussed telling Bishop's story to Charlie's mum and dad. Annie was particularly keen to tell her dad – the Hall Park legend, Johnny Cooper.

But there was a problem: they had no evidence.

True, Bishop could tell them about the conversation he had overheard but it would be his word against Di Santos'.

Di Santos was too clever to be caught like that, they knew.

He was too cunning.

They decided to deal with the problem themselves.

And the plan worked perfectly.

Being constantly surrounded by Magpies – with help from Joe and Bishop – meant the boy wonder was safe.

The gang kept their eyes peeled for danger but there had not been even a hint of trouble throughout the week.

Every night Charlie had stayed home with his parents, who were delighted to have their eldest boy watching TV with them.

It made a nice change rather than him practising football at the park.

His younger brother Harry was happy too – he had a rotten cold and hadn't been allowed out to play for more than a week.

And he loved seeing his brother's 'bodyguards' turn up.

Charlie found the attention embarrassing. But he did not say anything.

It felt like he was being babysat – by his own friends. Yet Charlie knew it was for his own good.

It was Friday night, the night before the big match.

The doorbell rang as Charlie sprawled on his bed. He had just finished an hour of physiotherapy. His chest, thankfully, was clear.

A few seconds later, Peter bounced into Charlie's room. He didn't knock, he never did.

"Alright, Smudger?"

Peter had a long list of nicknames for Charlie. He could never stick to using just one or two.

Charlie sat up to make space on the bed for his mate.

Peter jumped on to the duvet and picked the latest football magazine by Charlie's bed.

"So ... all set for tomorrow?"

Charlie smiled. "Yes. Dad is driving me to the game at 12.30pm so we can get there early. Do you want a lift?"

Peter lived with his dad. He worked as a plumber and often had to work when the football was on.

"Yes please. That would be great. My dad is going to the game but … he has work first."

Peter's voiced tailed off. He thought for a second. "Shall I come round for about 11am? We can put some early practice in?"

"Sounds great," replied Charlie. "I'll be glad when all this is over."

Peter grabbed his friend in a headlock.

"One more day, Charleston, and then you're going to win us the league – and get signed by the Premier League."

"Maybe." Charlie replied as he pushed his friend away.

Scouts from United and City had spoken to his dad this week.

But there had been no contact yet from the Blues, the team Charlie supported, despite every other Premier League club showing an interest.

Charlie felt a flutter of nerves in his stomach.

He had lost count of how many times he had prayed the Blues would come to watch him on Saturday.

Surely they would come to the game that everyone was talking about?

"Earth to Charlie Fry!"

Peter waved a hand in front of Charlie's face.

"Sorry, I … was just thinking about the game."

Peter edged along the bed.

"Yeah, that's understandable. Now we've got past Di Santos's traps and plots, we just have to beat his gang on the pitch."

Charlie flopped back down on the bed. "Yeah, and

facing Joe isn't going to be easy, is it?"

Peter nodded: "No, it is not. He is some player. It is going to be seriously strange."

Like Bishop, Joe played for Rovers.

Their best friend would be lining up against them in goal tomorrow. None of them, including Joe, knew how to feel about this.

Charlie scratched his chin: "Joe says they've got a whole bunch of new players too – a completely different team from when I was there.

"Di Santos is obsessed with winning so every time they lose or draw, he brings in a whole load of new players. Most of the guys I played with have left."

Peter sighed: "What a lovely fella. Nothing like a bit of loyalty, is there?"

The bedroom door opened. It was Charlie's dad Liam – with a serious look on his face.

He spoke quietly: "Harry is badly ill. An ambulance is coming. We've got to get to the hospital."

6. UNDER PRESSURE

Rexy paced up and down his filthy flat.

Things were not going to plan.

He had trailed the Boy Wonder for the past week with no success.

Charlie Fry was always with his annoying mates, which made things for more difficult than Rexy had first thought.

He checked his watch. It was 9.20pm. He had one of the local louts watching Fry's house this evening.

Rexy was beginning to get desperate. The game would kick off in fewer than 17 hours and Charlie Fry could not be on that pitch.

He needed the money.

He could start a new life with the cash, somewhere warm where people like Chell Di Santos would not bother him.

Rexy despised that man, but he did pay well. And Di Santos was paying extra for the Charlie Fry job.

Rexy needed extra help to get this done. But who could he trust?

Most of the usual Goon Squad was unsuitable.

Vinny P? Nope. He was too sensible to get involved in something like this.

Slippy Rolph? That old rascal moved away to London months ago to seek fame and fortune.

Rexy snapped his fingers in delight: Mambo Payne was the man for this.

He had not seen the big man in months but Mambo would be perfect.

A phone beeped, interrupting his thoughts.

The crook crossed the lounge in several bounds and saw the message waiting for him. It was Di Santos.

"Is it done?"

Rexy swallowed as he typed out a response.

"Not yet. Soon."

He sighed. Why did Di Santos make him nervous?

Rexy was used to dealing with bad people – villains of all shapes and sizes – but Di Santos gave him the creeps.

The phone beeped again.

"The game is tomorrow."

Rexy could feel sweat trickle down his back. He paused. He needed to pick the right words.

"It is all in hand."

He put the phone down again. A second later, it rang. He swallowed and answered without looking at the caller.

"Yes?"

Much to his surprise, it wasn't Di Santos. It was Big Andy – the teen who had been given the thankless job of watching the Fry household.

"Boss, there's an ambulance outside the Fry house."

Rexy's jaw fell open. "Is it Charlie?"

"I don't think so," replied Big Andy. "It looks like his brother is sick. There are lots of people going in and out of the house."

"Where is the Boy Wonder?"

"I can't ... wait ... I can see him! He's with that mate of his, Pete, I think. They're heading off together. Shall I follow them?"

"Of course, you fool! Don't let them out of your sight!"

Rexy flicked the phone shut before the boy could respond. His heart was pumping as the excitement began to grow.

This change of plans could play straight into his hands.

His phone beeped again.

Rexy's heart sank as he saw it was from Di Santos.

"Do not fail me."

7. CHANGE OF PLAN

Charlie heard his phone buzz.

He opened an eye, barely awake.

The room was not familiar. Where was he?

The boy wonder scanned his immediate surroundings. In the gloom it looked vaguely familiar, but he could not think where he had seen it before.

With one eye open, he sleepily grabbed the phone.

It was a message from his dad.

"Charlie, Harry is ok. Doctors keeping him in for a day but will be fine. I will meet you at the match later. Love, Dad."

Charlie suddenly felt wide awake. Of course, he knew where he was. It was Peter's house.

His mum and dad had taken his little brother to hospital last night. Harry had been struggling with a cough for a while and Charlie had sensibly given him a wide berth. But no-one had considered it to be too serious.

They had been wrong – and Harry had given them a scare last night, when he started finding it difficult to breathe.

Charlie had stayed at Peter's house while the rest of his family went to hospital.

Thankfully, Harry seemed to be on the mend.

Charlie breathed a sigh of relief as he fell back onto the pillow. He had not realised how worried he had been about his little brother.

The Boy Wonder checked his phone again: 6.03am. Less than eight hours to go until the match.

Charlie felt butterflies in his stomach. Nerves had been building but he had been completely forgotten with Harry falling ill.

Now he knew his brother was okay, they returned with a vengeance.

Today was the day. He would finally face Di Santos. He could do it. He would do it.

And if he did, Magpies would win the league.

It was one of the biggest days of his life.

"Fry, it is the middle of the night! What are you doing? Turn that stupid phone off."

Charlie smiled to himself. Peter was always so grumpy in the morning.

"I had a message from my dad."

Silence. Then Charlie could see the dark outline of his friend roll over in the bed on the other side of the room.

"And?"

"Harry is okay. They're keeping him in but only to keep an eye on him."

Peter sat up with a gentle stretch.

"Well, that's great news ... but I bet Harry will be gutted about missing the game.'"

Peter was right: Harry would be distraught at missing his brother's big match. He was his biggest fan – by a mile.

"Yes, he will but it can't be helped, can it?"

"No," replied Peter, waking up properly. "Hang on, is your dad still taking us to the game?"

Charlie shook his head even though it was too dark to be seen properly.

"No. He said he would meet us there. I guess he has other things on his mind. Can your dad give us a lift instead?"

"He is working. He was hoping to come for the second half but you know what his job is like – it's a nightmare with timings and things!"

Fully awake, Peter reached for his phone and began to type.

"What are you doing?"

Peter did not answer as his fingers flew over the screen. Finally he looked over at Charlie.

"What do you think? We've got to walk to the game … so we're going to need some help."

Charlie swung his legs out from under the duvet.

Any tiredness had disappeared.

"Good thinking! Who did you send that to?"

Peter shrugged. "Everybody."

"It is 6am!"

Charlie could imagine Peter's message waking up half the Magpies team. They would not be too happy to say the least.

"I know what the time is, Fry Up. And if they're not already up and preparing for today's game, then they are not the teammates – or friends – I thought they were."

As he spoke, Peter's phone started to vibrate as the responses began to flood in.

Middle of the night or not, they were not alone.

8. AWESOME FOURSOME

"Let's go."

Peter checked the front door. Happy it was locked, Peter stowed the keys inside his bag and turned to catch up with the others.

Emma, Toby and Charlie were halfway down the garden, near the small gate that led on to Peter's cul-de-sac.

Peter had been right.

Every member of Magpies had volunteered to walk with Charlie and Peter to the game. Even Joe – despite playing for Rovers today – had offered.

In the end, Peter decided a couple of people would be enough – he didn't want to ruin everyone's plans for the big day.

Emma, who was sent off in Magpies' last game, insisted on coming. She said it was one small way she could help the team out.

She still felt ashamed for allowing Adam Knight to get under her skin last week.

She had lashed out and paid the price. Emma had allowed the bully to win and let herself down.

Now Emma – one of Magpies' best players – was banned for the title decider. She felt terrible – and was desperate to make up for it.

And this was one way of doing that.

Toby was the final member of the gang.

Peter had planned to ask Wrecka to join them until Toby had turned up on the doorstep moments after Peter's dad had left for work.

After being woken by Peter's message, Toby had got up, grabbed the bag that he had packed the previous evening, and knocked on his mum's bedroom door.

He told her he was meeting friends before the game and he would see her at the stadium.

Before she could wake up, Toby had gone – grabbing only an apple for breakfast.

At 7am, he turned up at Peter's house.

Before anyone could ask, Toby simply said: "Charlie needs me. Nothing else matters."

The way he spoke stopped any argument. Even Peter, who never shied away from a good row, kept quiet.

Toby had been different since they had mistakenly accused him of being the football spy.

He seemed more determined than ever.

Emma had arrived at 10am and the friends began the two-mile walk from Peter's house to Hall Park's ground at 11am.

The game kicked off at 2pm. The walk took an hour but no-one wanted to be late today.

Toby would have left at 9am if he had been given the chance.

It was only when Charlie explained the stadium opened its doors two hours before kick-off that Toby agreed to leave later.

Now they were off.

The route from Peter's house to the ground was simple: through the familiar surroundings of The Rec, along Crickledon's winding high street before heading up Mewton Road past the town's old abandoned factories before reaching the stadium.

The friends did not talk much. They were lost in thought. The game loomed over them – it was so close.

Emma broke the silence.

"I want to stop at Thomas's."

"Why?" Peter asked.

"I want to buy a load of sweets, of course, for the celebrations later."

Peter sucked in air through his teeth. Charlie knew he did not like the idea of celebrating before anything had been won.

Emma, though, just wanted to help.

Charlie spoke before Peter could complain: "Great idea, Em. Make sure there's loads of toffees because everyone loves them."

Emma beamed with happiness.

"Sure thing, Boy Wonder."

Minutes later the boys were outside the iconic newsagents on the corner of Crickledon's busy high street.

Thomas's was the best sweet shop in town – with a selection to make your mouth drool as soon as you walked through the door.

Emma had already gone inside, leaving the others outside.

Peter kept looking round, constantly on his guard.

The high street was quiet but that didn't stop Peter scanning the street for danger.

"So what's the score going to be Toby?" Charlie was desperate to break the tension.

Toby grinned. "3-0. And it is only going to be that low because they've got a great goalkeeper!"

Charlie could feel the butterflies in his stomach.

Toby continued: "And then we're going to wave our trophy at Mr Di Santos and his management goons. And then…."

Toby's voice tailed off.

Charlie looked up: "And then … what?"

Toby blushed: "And then the Premier League might come calling for one of my best mates!"

Charlie did not get a chance to respond.

Peter's patience had snapped.

"WHAT IS SHE DOING IN THERE?!?!"

Charlie checked his phone. She had taken quite a while to buy some sweets.

Peter looked like he might explode: "I'm going in to find out what's going on. Will you be okay?"

Charlie laughed. "We will be fine. Go and find her."

Peter dumped his bag at Charlie's feet and marched into the newsagents – heading straight for the sweet section at the back of the shop.

Before he could get there, he spotted Emma. She was red-faced at the till with a small mountain of sweets in front of her.

"Oh Peter, I'm so sorry. I want to buy TEN POUNDS worth of sweets ... and this woman insists on counting every single one! It is taking forever."

The elderly woman behind the counter looked

sternly over her spectacles but said nothing.

"If you want to go, that's fine. I will catch you up, once I have proved to this lady that I am honest!"

The woman's tiny mouth somehow got even smaller with Emma's remarks.

Peter was so shocked by Emma's rage that he forgot his own anger.

"No, it is fine. I was just worried...."

Emma smiled brightly at him: "Awww, thank you. Are the others okay?"

Peter opened his mouth to respond but the scream outside stopped everyone in their tracks.

9. THE TRAP

Rexy watched the group of kids from a small café across the road.

He wore sunglasses so no-one could see where his attention was focused.

Everything was ready.

Big Andy had trailed behind the gang through the park. Now the children were in the high street, almost right in front of him.

It was quiet on Crickledon's shopping street.

Witnesses should not be a problem if they moved quickly.

The CCTV cameras overlooking the road had been broken overnight so there would be no footage for anyone to watch later.

All he needed was a chance. One mistake and he would get him.

Charlie, the girl and the small boy, who was called Toby, seemed oblivious to the danger.

Peter Bell, though, was a problem. He was always looking out for trouble, constantly watching and alert.

Rexy rubbed his trimmed beard.

Sweat was building on his brow. He pulled the paper napkin from the saucer in front of him and dabbed his forehead.

He was dressed fully in designer clothes, all black. Even the coffee in front of him was black.

He did not stand out. Nothing that would make people remember him if they were asked later on.

Rexy leaned forward.

The girl had disappeared into Thomas's newsagents – and had yet to reappear.

The others were waiting outside but seemed to be arguing.

Rexy felt the hairs stand up on his neck. He picked up his phone. The moment was close.

Mambo was parked around the corner in a layby outside a butchers shop and waited for the call.

He answered in one ring. "Yeah."

"Get the engine running, Mambo, and stay on the line."

"You got it, boss."

Rexy kept the phone to his ear and walked to the door of the empty coffee shop. His eyes never left Charlie Fry.

And then it happened.

Peter, of all people, disappeared into the shop too.

It left Charlie alone with his small friend Toby.

"Go, Mambo, go."

Rexy slipped the phone inside his jacket pocket as he emerged from the coffee shop.

Within seconds he was across the road.

He had waited a long time to capture Charlie Fry.

And that chance had finally arrived.

10. SNATCHED

It happened so quickly.

A man in a black suit appeared from nowhere and fell over Toby's kit bag.

As he crashed to the pavement, the stranger squealed and clutched his leg in agony.

Toby rushed over, apologising.

Charlie watched with confusion.

He stood above the man and, despite the sunglasses, could see most of his face.

It was clear he was not in any pain despite the loud complaining.

He was pretending.

In fact, he did not even look in Toby's direction. He was staring at Charlie instead.

As he apologised, Toby did not notice the firm grip on his arm.

Charlie's stomach lurched.

Something wasn't right.

Danger.

But it was too late.

"Toby…"

Two large hands grabbed Charlie underneath the armpits and yanked him into the air.

He tried to break free but was not strong enough.

Whoever had hold of him would not let go.

He could hear a car door opening as he was dragged away.

He screamed.

"Geeeerrrrooooffffffff meeeeeeeeee!"

Toby turned as Charlie screamed.

His eyes widened as he watched his friend being wrestled towards a red car by a big bald man.

Toby tried to move but the man on the pavement gripped his arm tightly.

He was not letting go.

Toby tried to lash out but the man easily caught the punch. Toby had been captured too.

Charlie watched as the man in black scooped up his friend.

His eyes flicked to the shop door – surely Peter and Emma had heard the screams?

It was empty.

Charlie tried to shout again but tape was pushed over his mouth.

Seconds later, he was thrown head-first into the car boot.

Toby followed moments later. Then it all went black.

The boot was slammed shut. Several doors opened and closed.

As the engine started, they heard a window smash and a loud thud against the side of the car.

Peter.

Emma.

Charlie's heart soared at the arrival of his friends –

but the car began to move away and soon the banging faded to nothing.

Lying in the dark and unable to speak, Charlie knew exactly who was behind this.

Chell Di Santos had finally lost the plot.

11. PANIC

Peter watched the red car disappear along the high street.

Then it was gone.

His arm had already begun to throb where he had desperately rammed into the side of the moving car.

He had been too late.

"Noooooooooo!!!!"

Emma screamed as the sound of the car's engine faded away.

As soon as they'd heard the scream, they had ditched the sweets and ran.

Peter emerged from the shop to see Toby being shoved into the boot by some guy he'd never seen before. He guessed Charlie was already in there.

Peter had been fast – but not quick enough.

He had launched himself at the vehicle's rear window and hoped to stop the car. Despite making a loud bang, it did not work.

He had simply bounced off.

As Peter fell to the pavement, Emma tried to

unlock the car boot and free the boys.

But it could not be done while the car was moving.

With a spin of the tyres, the car was gone – whisking Charlie and Toby away with it.

The friends stood in silence.

"Peter, who are those people? What are we going to do?"

Emma had her hands on her head. Peter could see the tears beginning to flow.

He did not answer.

Peter kept looking down the high street – where the car had disappeared moments before.

"It's him."

"Who?"

Peter sighed. "Di Santos. Bishop warned us, didn't he? We agreed to protect the Boy Wonder and we've failed him."

Emma's mouth dropped open.

"Oh no. We've let him down. What about the big match? We'll be two people down – at least!"

Emma began to sob.

By now, the woman at the newsagents and an old man with a shopping trolley were approaching with looks of confusion on their faces.

Peter put an arm around Emma.

He whispered: "We still have two hours. We will rescue them both. I promise."

Emma turned to face him: "Do you really think so?"

Peter gritted his teeth: "Of course. We never give up."

They hugged but Peter's mind was racing.

It had been easy to say but he had no idea what to do next.

12. A SHORT TRIP

Space inside the car boot was limited.

Charlie could barely move with Toby squashing him.

"Toby, can you reach the lock?"

"Yes, I can … wait a minute … no, there's nothing there."

"Drat. Can you move? You're killing my legs."

Toby shifted a fraction.

"That's all I can do, Charlie. There isn't much room down this end either."

It did help a little. The pins and needles eased slightly.

"Charlie, who are these people? What's going on?"

The Boy Wonder shrugged and then realised it was too dark for Toby to see his response.

"No idea. Let's …"

He stopped. He could hear the men talking. Charlie strained to hear the conversation.

"Charlie?" whispered Toby.

"Ssshhhh! They're talking. I can hear them."

Toby fell quiet.

Slowly over the hum of the engine, Charlie could hear the discussion taking place in the front part of the car.

"… I'm just not happy, boss. That's all I'm saying. They're just little kids. I dunno … it … just seems wrong."

"Look, Mambo. It is nothing. We are not going to hurt them."

Charlie let out a small sigh of relief.

The second voice spoke again: "All we have to do is keep these two away from Hall Park's ground for the next four hours or so.

"Once it reaches 4.30pm, we've done it. Then we can let the little runts go. After that we pick up the rest of our cash and I am out of here."

Charlie's heart was beating like a drum. The football! They planned to stop him and Toby from playing in the big match.

Mambo spoke again: "I dunno, Rexy. It still seems wrong. I think we're gonna be on camera and every fink after that stunt back there."

Rexy laughed. It sounded heartless, Charlie thought.

"Yes, we may be famous for a week or two.

"I would suggest you get out of town as soon as we're done. It will calm down soon."

"This is not what we agreed! This is out of control, innit?" Mambo's voice rose as his temper threatened to boil over.

When Rexy replied, his voice was calm: "We had no choice: it was now or never. And Di Santos was clear that it had to be done."

Charlie froze. He should have known.

"Charlie, did you hear that?!" Toby could not hide his amazement.

"Ssshhh!"

The voices were still talking.

Mambo sounded calmer. "So what's the plan then, Gaffer?"

Rexy chuckled.

"It is simple. We are going to take these Herberts to the last place any one would think of looking for them.

"And, best of all, by the time they manage to find them; I'll be on a beach in Spain."

Charlie stopped listening.

They had to get out.

Time was against them.

"Toby, can you reach my coat pocket? My phone is in there."

13. DIVIDED

Peter's phone made a noise.

He ignored it.

Both he and Emma were in the middle of a heated conversation with Joe.

Joe turned up five minutes ago – and he was fuming.

"How could you let this happen? You only had to watch him this morning!

"All our hard work is wasted … because you were buying a mountain of penny sweets! I could swing for both of you."

Unless Adam Knight was involved, Joe rarely got angry.

Peter was the hothead, not Joe.

But not today.

"I'm sorry...." Peter's voice trailed off. There were no words: he had been responsible for Charlie and he had failed.

His face burning with shame, Peter turned his back on Joe and Emma.

How could this have happened? They had been so careful.

He could see a group of adults talking inside the shop. He knew they were contacting the police.

It was the last thing they needed.

The game was taking place in less than two hours.

Magpies needed Charlie for the game.

Where were those idiots taking him?

He pulled out his phone to check a map of the town.

It may tell him the best place to head towards. It was a desperate move but he simply did not what else to do.

A flashing light jogged his memory.

He had forgotten a message had arrived a few moments ago.

Peter gasped. It was from Charlie.

Peter could feel his hand tremble.

He looked at the words and frowned.

He rubbed his eyes and looked again. No, he wasn't seeing things.

The words made no sense.

"Hepl us. Di Santps."

Peter turned back to the others and thrust the phone under Joe's nose.

The message on the screen shone brightly.

Joe and Emma studied it for a second.

"When did you get this?" Joe's voice was barely a whisper.

"Just now! It makes no sense though, does it?"

Joe beckoned Emma and Peter closer. He didn't want the grown-ups to overhear them.

"It is obvious, isn't it?"

Emma and Peter looked at him with blank faces.

"No."

Joe sighed.

"They want us to help them ... and Chell Di Santos is behind this."

Emma gasped.

"What should we do?" Peter's voice lacked its usual confidence.

Joe shrugged.

"Let's ring him."

14. NO ESCAPE

"I've sent it, Charlie. I couldn't see the screen so I hope it made sense."

"Well done, Toby. Keep hold of the phone. If you put it back in my pocket and it falls out, then we're done for."

"Okay, Fry-inho. I won't let it go – no matter what."

Charlie could not help but admire Toby. He had been thrown into the car boot by two burly men due to his friendship with Charlie.

It was cramped and hot. It was also pretty scary.

Yet he did not complain or cry.

Instead, he refused to be frightened by anyone.

Charlie did not know anyone braver than Toby Grace.

He was not the biggest or the strongest but there was no-one else he would rather have on his side.

The car had stopped a few minutes ago.

Charlie had heard two cars door slam shut, which meant both men were away from the car.

It did not matter. Both boys were so cramped in the boot they could not even move, let alone plot an escape.

The phone was their only hope.

They waited for a response.

Silence.

"Come on, Peter," whispered Toby.

Then the boys heard a voice outside.

It was the one who had been worried about what they'd done – Mambo. They could tell from the accent. He had a thick Crickledon drawl; like a farmer would sound.

"I've checked it, boss. It's clear. There's hardly anyone …" Mambo struggled to find the right words, "… about here either."

"Good work. Let's move them now, nice and quick. You take the little one and I'll grab the Boy Wonder."

"You got it."

The car boot opened and light flooded in.

They had only been in darkness for perhaps ten minutes – probably less – but Charlie felt blinded by the glare.

Instinctively he turned his head away from the brightness.

Seconds later, the weight on his legs disappeared: Toby had been roughly pulled out of the car.

He felt a pair of large hands grab his sweatshirt. He tried to push them away but the grip was like iron.

Then he was yanked with such force that he felt the air disappear from his lungs.

He began coughing and could not stop.

He could see Toby struggling with the beefy guy in front.

Charlie did not have the energy to fight back.

The coughing was getting worse. It felt like an explosion in his chest every time he tried to clear his throat.

And the guy's grip stopped him getting enough air into his chest to sort the problem out.

After what seemed to be a lifetime, they stopped and the man threw Charlie on to the ground alongside Toby.

Charlie gasped for breath as Toby spoke for both of them.

"He is ill, you morons! Do you know how serious it is if he falls ill? What are you playing at? Let us go."

Charlie saw the man called Rexy give Toby a menacing stare.

"Shut up, you little turd. No-one cares what you think. Don't speak again unless I tell you to."

Toby opened his mouth but stopped as Rexy stamped on his ankle.

"I mean it. Nothing more."

Toby kept quiet.

Mambo appeared from nowhere. "Boss, we're in. The door is open."

And then disaster struck.

Charlie's phone rang.

Amid the coughing, Charlie saw Rexy smile wickedly.

"Awww. Looks like no-one is getting rescued today."

It rang.

And rang.

Finally Rexy leaned forward and plucked the smartphone from Toby's hand.

In a swift move, he threw the phone to the floor,

where it shattered into a thousand pieces.

"Mambo, we nearly messed this up. Get them inside and check for phones, watches or tablets.

"Destroy anything that can be used to contact the outside world. The last thing we need is anyone trying to save them."

Mambo grabbed Toby first and carried him inside the wooden hut, leaving Charlie alone on the floor.

Rexy pulled out his own phone and began to type a message out.

None of them saw the teenager watching across the park, using his black guitar case to keep his large frame hidden.

15. DISCOVERED

Peter, Emma and Joe waited for someone to answer the phone.

Nothing happened.

"Come on, Charlie. Answer the phone!"

The ringing continued but there was still no answer.

Then in a flash, the call stopped.

"What happened?" Joe looked confused.

Peter shook his head. "No idea. Let me try again."

He dialled the number but this time it went to answerphone. Peter hung up and rang again. The same result.

"They've got his phone." Joe said what they were all thinking.

Emma chimed in. "What do we do next?"

Neither of them responded.

How could they help Charlie and Toby? They didn't even know where they were.

"We could confront Chell Di Santos," said Peter.

Joe shook his head. "And say what? We know

nothing – the only proof we have is a poorly spelt message.

"And that doesn't even confirm it is him behind all this. No, that's no good."

They stood in silence. How could they help their friends?

Then a strange voice rang out.

"Thank goodness I've found you. I was trying to get to Hall Park."

Peter, Joe and Emma looked up.

Stephen Cleatman, the Colts central midfielder who had run rings around them in the previous game, was sitting on a bike five metres away.

Despite Magpies winning the game, Cleatman was the best player on the pitch. Yet he was more interested in music than football.

And sure enough, he had his trusty guitar strapped to his back.

Peter stepped forward. "You okay, Cleat?"

Cleatman looked exhausted. His shaggy hair dripped with sweat and his T-shirt had dark patches on it. He looked like he'd run a marathon.

Cleatman nodded: "I didn't have your numbers or I would have rung. Your pals – Charlie and the other guy – are over the other side of town."

"Toby?" Joe replied.

Cleatman nodded: "Yeah, that's him. Anyway, I've just seen two goons lugging them into the clubhouse.

"They seemed pretty nasty … and Charlie seemed to be coughing a lot."

Emma asked the obvious question.

"Where are they?"

Cleatman said: "They're at Manor Park. Charlie and Toby are at the home of Magpies."

16. LIES

Joe stood and looked at the usual faces: Peter, Emma, Wrecka, Mudder, Annie and Flem.

Bishop was next to Peter, the final member of the group.

There were no smiles or mucking about.

The usual banter was missing. Everyone had a serious expression.

It was crunch time.

A round of phone calls and messages had changed everyone's plans.

Now they stood on a small patch of grass next to Crickledon's war memorial.

They could see where Toby and Charlie were taken: Thomas's newsagent was over the road.

The police had arrived a few minutes ago and would soon want to speak to Emma and Peter.

The gang needed a fresh plan – and they had to be quick.

Joe had told them everything Cleatman had seen: two men had carried Toby and Charlie into the

Manor Park clubhouse about 45 minutes ago.

Joe continued: "It is clever. Why would anyone go near Manor Park today?

"It will be completely deserted.

"Their phones are out of action. We have to get over there – now."

The game kicked off in less than an hour. It was going to be tight.

"I'm going."

"Me too."

Peter and Emma were both determined to make up for letting those thugs take their friends.

Joe shook his head.

"No. You'll have to speak to the police. That could take a while – and we need you to help at the match, Peter."

Peter did not understand. "What are you talking about?"

Annie butted in: "It is obvious! Even if we do rescue him, Charlie and Toby will miss the game. We need to make sure that doesn't happen."

"Er … right," said Peter, who still did not look too sure.

Joe continued: "We need two volunteers to go and save Charlie and Toby."

"Me." Bishop stepped forward.

He was wearing his Rovers kit but he had clearly no intention of playing for Chell Di Santos's team.

"Me too." Annie had that look again: no-one wanted to argue with her.

Wrecka was the only one brave enough to disagree. "Annie, we can't afford to lose you too. We're already short of players."

Silence.

Everyone waited for her response.

Finally she spoke: "I can't leave him. I should have been there…."

Emma gave her friend a gentle squeeze. "Annie, you've got to play. Charlie would want that."

Emma turned to the rest: "This is my mistake. I am not playing anyway so no-one is going to miss me. Please let me go and put things right."

Several nodded their agreement.

Joe smiled: "It isn't your fault, Em. But you're right: you're the perfect choice.

"Both of you should go now.

"If you can't get them out, don't put yourselves at risk. Ring the police."

Bishop grunted: "Understood. Come on Em, let's save our mates."

Within 30 seconds, the pair had disappeared out of sight, heading towards Manor Park.

The gang watched them disappear and turned back to face Joe.

He spoke slowly: "Even if they do manage to save Toby and Charlie, they will still miss the game."

Wrecka scratched his head: "What are we going to do?"

Joe took a deep breath before speaking.

"Without Charlie, Magpies would find it tough. But without Charlie, Toby, Emma, and perhaps Peter too, they've no chance."

Wrecka nodded.

"Yep, we've only got two subs. So the best we can hope for is starting the game with only nine players…."

"This is not right," Joe replied.

The goalkeeper's cheeks turned pink with anger.

Regardless of his team, there could be no doubt over which side Joe was on.

"Rovers have lost Bishop – but we have got loads of subs.

"It'll make no difference.

"So we have to give the missing Magpies players as much time as possible to get back to the match."

Joe motioned for the others to move in closer, which they did immediately.

"I've got an idea. This is what we're going to do."

17. AWAITING GLORY

Chell Di Santos checked his watch: an hour until kick-off.

He could feel sweat. He rarely sweated and did not enjoy feeling damp.

Everything rested on the next few hours.

Glory awaited – if Rexy could fulfil his end of the bargain.

He stood on the Hall Park pitch alone.

It was perfect, like a carpet.

He snorted.

Football was not like this when he was growing up.

Matches were played in muddy fields where the white ball was always a horrible shade of brown.

The weather was fine – it was a glorious spring day.

He would be the only person wearing a winter coat today.

He did not care.

He was Chell Di Santos.

He was different.

He stood out from the crowd.

The Rovers manager took a deep breath to soak up the familiar match smells.

Today was the day. Spectators had begun to fill up the ground.

No-one wanted to miss the big showdown: The Football Boy Wonder versus The Demon Football Manager.

Di Santos knew what they called him. It did not bother him.

He shook his head a fraction.

The English were a strange bunch.

Almost every country in the world loved football but they were obsessive.

The Crickledon Telegraph yesterday claimed the match was a sell-out.

Crazy, he thought to himself.

Apart from parents, who would watch a youth football match?

Normally, hardly anyone would be interested.

Today was not normal though – not in the slightest.

Apparently the club had sold 10,000 tickets for the game.

It was the only time in Hall Park's history the ground had sold out without the men's first team playing.

In an hour, the terraces would be heaving.

His phone rang as Rexy's name popped up on the screen.

Surely he could not fail again.

"Yes?"

There was no greeting. This was strictly business.

Both would throw their phones away after the match, removing any trace of contact between them.

"We've got him."

"At last. Keep him for another three hours until the match is over."

"Got it. We've got one of his friends too."

"Why?"

Rexy's voice remained calm: "Some boy called Toby. There was no other way. We've kept him with Fry so there's no problem."

Di Santos shrugged. As long as the Boy Wonder was out of the picture, he did not care.

"Just keep them hidden. No slip ups."

The response was instant. "Mambo is sitting outside the door. No-one is getting in or out of there unless I say so."

Di Santos replied: "Good, very good. One last thing: does the little ... nuisance know about my involvement?"

"No."

"Excellent. Make sure it stays that way."

He closed the phone without another word and slipped it back into his coat pocket.

Then he let out a sigh of relief.

The Hall Park Rovers Under-13s boss could feel the tension leave his body.

Without Charlie Fry, Magpies would not threaten his team.

They were already missing Emma Tysoe after her red card against Colts and now, thanks to Rexy, their star player would be absent too.

Di Santos smirked.

Everything was going to plan.

He could only imagine Barney Payne's reaction

when the Magpies manager discovered he had lost half his pathetic team.

He would, no doubt, try to call the game off.

No chance.

The local rivals would go head to head today to decide the winners of the Under-13s league.

And with the Boy Wonder mysteriously absent, Rovers would have an easy stroll to the title.

Yes, today was going to be glorious, Di Santos reminded himself, as he headed back to the changing room.

18. THE FEW

Barney Payne looked around the room.

It was half empty and virtually silent.

The only sound came from Paul Greaves who nervously bounced a ball against a wall.

No-one spoke.

There was only ten minutes to go until kick-off.

Something was wrong.

Most of the Magpies team were missing.

They were never late.

And Barney knew his players would not have been late for this match, no matter what.

There had to be another explanation.

He scratched his chin as he looked around.

Only Billy Savage, Greavesy, Theo Tennison, Gary Bradshaw and Jimmy Welford had taken part in the warm-up.

He had sent Ted the physio to look for the missing players.

It was a shot in the dark but what else could he do?

He had to try something.

Where was Wrecka? He was the team's captain.

What about Charlie? The boy with golden shooting boots rarely missed a game.

Or Annie? Or the others?

Barney closed his eyes.

He could hear the hum of the packed stadium above.

In all his years, he could not remember Hall Park being so full.

Supporters had turned out in their thousands – and they were going to be hugely disappointed.

It was the biggest game of the season and Magpies did not have enough players to even start the match.

The game.

The title.

The league.

It was the most important match in his career – and it was over before it had even started.

He suddenly felt old. Barney had seen thousands of children play for Hall Park's junior teams over the last 30 years.

He could have retired years ago but his love of football made that a non-starter. But today he felt like someone had punched him in the stomach.

"Boss?"

Barney jumped.

Gary Bradshaw stood in front of him with a look of concern on his face.

The boy cleared his throat and repeated: "Boss?"

"Yes ... sorry ... I ..."

Barney stopped himself. What could he say?

He was sorry but the team's hard work was wasted?

The dream of winning the league was over before the match had even started?

He paused for a moment and then replied carefully: "Yes, Gary. What's up?"

"Where is everyone, boss? It's nearly kick-off and we've only got half a team. Is something going on?"

Barney could see the Magpies players looking at him. Greavesy had picked the ball up and tucked it under his arm.

They looked worried to death. What could he say to them?

He glanced at the clock.

He swallowed, despite his throat being bone dry, and prepared to tell them the truth: he was heading over to the Rovers' changing room and would forfeit the game because Magpies did not have enough players.

In about three seconds, he was going to destroy their dreams, everything they had worked so hard for.

"Are they okay?" Jimmy chimed in from the far side of the changing room.

Silence.

"We're fine." Wrecka's voice boomed out before the away changing room door was even fully open.

Barney felt a surge of joy.

The Magpies captain strode into the room closely followed by Annie, Mudder and Flem.

Barney's smile faltered a tad as the door closed.

They were still missing players.

Barney stood in front of Wrecka and put two hands on his shoulders. He looked the boy directly in the eye.

"What has happened, Mike? Are you all okay? And where are the others?"

Barney could not keep the concern out of his voice.

Wrecka bit his lip: "It is a long story, boss. The others are coming but they won't be here for kick-off."

"Why? What on earth is going on?"

Wrecka turned his gaze towards Annie, who gave the briefest of nods.

His attention returned to Barney.

"They've taken Charlie and Toby. We know where they are.

"Brian Bishop and Emma have gone to rescue them.

"Peter is talking to the police about the kidnapping: he should be here in a short while."

Barney's mouth fell open.

When he spoke, it was a whisper. "Who did this?"

Wrecka could not hide his anger.

"Who do you think? Who would benefit most from Charlie missing the big match?"

Barney shook his head. "Di Santos? Surely not?"

You could hear a pin drop in the changing room. Everyone stood still, amazed at the conversation.

Annie ended the silence.

"Believe us, boss. It is the truth. Now we have to give Charlie, Toby and Peter as much time as possible to get back here.

"For a while, we're only going to have nine players but we've got a plan. This is what we are going to do."

19. NEVER GIVE UP

BANG!

The door rattled as it was thumped.

"Cut that out, you idiots. No-one is gonna be coming out unless we decide, so pipe down!"

It was Mambo. The gruff accent was a giveaway.

Toby and Charlie glared silently at the locked door.

They had tried force it open using their combined weight but the lock remained firmly shut.

And Rexy and Mambo were watching on the other side anyway.

Time was running out.

It was only a few minutes until kick-off.

Instead of preparing for the game of their lives at Hall Park, they were stuck in the familiar surroundings of Manor Park.

They had been bundled into Barney's office and the sturdy door had been slammed behind them.

The friends heard the lock turn but thought they could wedge it open if both of them pushed against it.

It had not worked and now the boys were

beginning to get desperate.

Barney's office was small and dark.

The only light came from a sky-light in the roof.

They could not reach it. Even if they stood on the desk with one on the other's shoulders, they would still be too short.

Toby dropped to his knees and began to search for a trap-door; an escape route; anything that could help them get out.

Charlie held a finger to his lips to quieten Toby.

The goons were obviously listening to them. They did not want to raise suspicions.

Toby understood and continued his search more carefully.

Charlie rifled through the desk.

Surely there must be something here to help them?

It was just ancient newspapers, old football programmes and paperwork.

He smiled as he thought about Barney's chaotic style of management.

The grin faded. Barney would only have half a team today.

Knowing the Magpies manager, he would not be worried about the game – it was his players he would be concerned about.

Toby whispered: "Charlie? Are you okay? Have you found something?"

He was covered in dust.

Charlie tapped his front teeth.

"No, I haven't found anything that can help us."

Toby pushed down the hairs sticking up at the back of his head.

As usual, they sprang up again as soon as his hand moved away. "Me neither."

Charlie spluttered.

The dust caught in his throat. He perched on the edge of the desk and tried to keep his breathing under control.

"You okay?"

"Yeah," replied Charlie, "but we're going to miss the football today. There's no way out – other than the door."

"Don't say that!" Toby looked around with a sense of desperation.

Finally he looked up at the skylight in the distant rafters of the roof. "Could we reach that, do you reckon?"

Charlie followed his pal's gaze.

He knew the answer.

The window was tiny but Charlie and Toby were hardly huge.

They might be able to squeeze through if they sucked their tummies in.

It looked filthy – like it had not been opened in years.

The problem was height. They would need to climb a long way – and do it without Rexy and Mambo hearing them as well.

Tricky.

Charlie could feel his breathing return to normal.

"I don't think so. It is too high.

"But what choice have we got? We have to try."

20. HELPING HAND

"Come on, Bishop! Not much further."

Emma could see Manor Park's welcome sign in the distance. Bishop lagged 20 metres behind.

He didn't answer. They had raced across town in record time.

The streets were deserted, with most people at Hall Park.

The pair stopped as they reached the park gates and tried to catch their breath.

They had done the easy bit. The next part was trickier. How were they going to rescue their friends?

Emma checked her watch. "The game is about to start. We need to do something – quickly. What do you reckon?"

Bishop grimaced at the stitch in his side. "I dunno. Let's walk down by the trees and see if we can suss out what's going on."

They began to move along the treeline, as Bishop suggested. They did not want to raise the kidnappers' suspicions.

There were no crowds to blend in with. Like the town, the park was empty too.

"That's the car!"

Emma excitedly pointed in the direction of the car park, where a red car stood alone.

She recognised it immediately – the same vehicle that had swept Charlie and Toby away.

"Cleatman was right: they are here!"

Their eyes moved to the club-house. Magpies' pitch stood between them and the old building that held their friends.

Some idiot had forgotten to take down the nets after the last game. Manor Park looked ready for a match – except it was deserted.

Bishop scanned the wooden decking in front of the clubhouse.

The double doors were closed. Every now and then a face appeared against the glass.

Bishop elbowed Emma.

"Ow! What are you doing?"

He put a finger to his lips. "Ssssshhh. Look at the doors closely. Someone is watching them."

They waited for one of the crooks to show their faces again.

"There!" Emma pointed as a white shape appeared in the frosty glass.

The face disappeared again. Emma and Bishop crouched behind a bush and looked at each other.

"We can't get them out that way. Is there another way into the clubhouse?"

Emma's nose wrinkled up. "I ... can't remember. I don't know ... perhaps there is. Let's try round the back?"

Bishop nodded.

"Yep, but let's stick to the undergrowth again. They are keeping watch so we need to be sneaky."

It did not take them long.

Soon they were sitting in a patch of brambles near the back of the clubhouse. Emma had been right: there was no back door.

"What are we going to do now?" Emma could not hide her despair.

Then they saw it together: a small hand bashing against a filthy sky light near the top of the roof.

It had to be Charlie and Toby.

Bishop stood up and hauled Emma with him.

"What are we going to do?

"We're going to rescue our friends, just like we planned."

21. TIME

Joe stood in the Rovers goalmouth as the referee prepared to blow the whistle and start the match.

It had been a crazy day.

And it was not finished yet.

The crowd was huge. He had always dreamed of playing in front of a full house at Hall Park. Now it was happening.

The Charlie Fry factor.

The interest in his best mate was incredible. Joe's stomach flipped as he thought of his trapped friends but he pushed it away.

They would be fine, he told himself.

He needed to focus on the plan.

He scanned the benches of the two teams: his Rovers team was packed with substitutes and the back room team while Magpies' was empty – Barney and Ted stood on the side-line alone.

He could see Rovers' reserve goalkeeper Sam Walker, known as Peppermint, on the bench. He looked fed up.

Peppermint used to play for Magpies but had been lured away by Chell Di Santos.

But, instead of becoming a regular for Rovers, he had been stuck on the bench while Magpies soared up the table.

With Joe running so late, he was in line to start the biggest game of the season.

But when Joe turned up at the last minute, Chell Di Santos promptly gave the starting place back to his number one and poor Sam returned dejectedly to his familiar position on the bench.

The Rovers boss was ruthless.

The Hall Park Stadium clock said the game was already running 14 minutes late.

Joe hid a smirk by pretending to cough. The plan was working so far.

It was pretty simple: they would delay the match as much as possible to give Peter, Charlie and Toby a chance to take part in the match.

Magpies had been forced to change kits after Joe and Rovers captain Seamus Houseman had complained to referee about being unable to see their green shirts.

Apart from Joe, Seamus was the only Rovers player who knew about the plan. Last year, Seamus had been a bully – one of Adam Knight's gang of thugs.

But he had changed. Now Joe trusted only him and Bishop in the Rovers team – and Bishop would soon be leaving.

Magpies, it turned out, did not have a second strip so they had borrowed Rovers' spares – an orange top like the Dutch national team.

The pre-match handshakes had been hilarious.

Wrecka and Annie had chatted to every Rovers player; Flem kept asking about haircuts; Mudder wanted to talk about video games.

Instead of shaking hands, the Magpies players spoke with the Rovers team ignoring the confused looks.

The goalkeeper chuckled as he overheard Wrecka ask the referee where he had bought his whistle.

Brilliant.

But it was not enough.

The game was about to kick off and Magpies still only had nine players. There was no sign yet of Charlie, Peter and Toby.

Joe scowled.

He knew Magpies could not hold out without equal numbers. He certainly did not want to lose – but he wanted a fair game.

Chell Di Santos did not play fairly.

This was cheating. He wanted to win but not this way.

His buddies needed more time. They would make it back, Joe reminded himself, but they needed a chance.

The ref's whistle blew.

The crowd roared. The moment had arrived.

Wrecka lumped the ball forward towards no-one in particular. Magpies had stuck Flem up front but he was nowhere near the ball.

Joe sauntered out of goal and claimed the loose ball. Seamus ran towards him with a little nod of the head.

Joe understood. He held on to the ball until Flem got much closer and then rolled the ball out to Seamus, immediately putting the defender under pressure.

Seamus controlled the ball and turned slowly, inviting Flem to close him down. The Magpies player did not need a second invitation.

At the last moment, Seamus tried to make a clearance.

It did not work. Instead the ball crashed into Flem's outstretched knee and cannoned towards the Rovers goal.

Joe watched the ball float towards the empty net and moved backwards.

He covered the ground quickly and realised the ball would go wide by a couple of centimetres.

But it did not matter whether the ball was going in or not.

It was the perfect opportunity.

His outstretched hand knocked the ball behind for a corner. At the same time, Joe flung out his left boot and clipped the goalpost.

"OOWWWWW!"

Joe covered up his face and curled up into a small ball. In the distance he could hear Flem and Seamus calling for the physio.

He clutched his leg and groaned in fake agony as he waited for the medics to arrive.

"AARRGGHHHH!"

His performance should waste a few more precious minutes and give his friends a little more time to make the match at least.

22. BREAK OUT

"Be careful, Bish!"

Emma whispered as he clambered on to the roof of the clubhouse.

He was trying to be careful but it was not easy.

The wooden roof groaned under his weight. Bishop winced at the noise.

He was not sure it would hold his weight.

Bishop dropped down to his knees and began to crawl.

The new position meant his weight was spread across the roof and put less pressure on the ancient timber.

He was now halfway towards the skylight.

Bishop could no longer see the hands tapping the sky-light but it did not matter. He knew they were in Barney's office.

He had to get them out.

Finally Bishop pulled his body up to the small window. It was tight. He would not be able to fit through it.

Luckily, Toby and Charlie were a lot smaller than him.

Bishop tried to lift the skylight. It would not budge. A rusty latch on the inside stopped it opening.

The boys would need to release the catch before it could be opened. He peered inside.

Charlie and Toby were talking to each other – far below. They were not looking upwards.

There was no time to waste. Bishop had no other choice: he banged on the skylight as hard as he could.

"Bishop, what on earth are you doing?" Emma hissed from below. She sounded mad.

Bishop ignored her. He watched the boys turn to the door, thinking the noise had come from there.

He banged again.

It was Toby who looked up first. His eyes opened with disbelief as he pointed in Bishop's direction.

Bishop signalled he would open the skylight if they could release the latch.

It did not take them long to figure out what he wanted.

Within seconds, Charlie was back on Toby's shoulders.

Centimetre by centimetre, Charlie's fingers moved closer to the latch that would free them.

"Come on, Fry!" Bishop whispered through the glass.

Charlie's fingers scraped the lock. It still did not budge.

Bishop sat, unable to help. He could see the effort on Charlie's face as he strained to set the latch free.

Another thought sprung into Bishop's mind.

Charlie was at full stretch. Even if they got the window open, Bishop would have to help pull them out.

And the window was so tiny that he only had enough space to use one arm.

Even though the boys were small, Bishop doubted he could lift them with one arm.

They needed something else. Something they could climb up. He looked around in desperation. The rescue attempt would fail without help.

His eyes scanned the empty park: the deserted car park; the woods they had crept along; the pitch.

Bishop looked down at Emma.

"Em?"

"Yes?"

"We're going to need one of those goal nets. Grab it as fast as you can please and throw it up to me!"

Whoever had forgotten to take down the nets after Magpies' last home game may just have saved the team's star player.

Emma shot off without another word.

She raced towards the nearest goal and began to frantically rip the patched-up net away from the crossbar.

Bishop hoped the net would hold the boys' weight.

He turned back to the skylight. Charlie's fingers were clasped around the rusty lock. Slowly the latch was beginning to move.

"Come on Charlie!" Bishop whispered again.

A final push and the latch came free. With a huge yank, Bishop opened the skylight and grinned at his mates below.

"Alright lads? Fancy being stuck in here when there's a football match to be won."

Charlie looked exhausted. "Bish, I can't reach you. We're going to need something to help us out."

He swayed slightly. Toby was obviously struggling to keep Charlie on his shoulders.

"Hold on. Emma is coming with one of the goal nets. You can climb up that. You'll be out soon, I promise."

"Bish!"

He turned and saw Emma with the net in her arms. She was trying to push it up the wall of the clubhouse but was not getting far.

Bishop looked back to Charlie.

"I'll be back in a moment! Stay right there!"

He slid back down to the edge of the roof and thrust out a hand. Emma flung the net in his direction, and he grabbed it.

"Got it!"

Bishop lugged the net behind him as he crawled back towards the open window.

It took longer this time. The net was surprisingly heavy. Bishop could feel sweat drip off his nose with the effort.

"Bish! Hurry!"

With a heave, Bishop lugged the net over the opening and let half the material drop down into the room.

He plonked himself on to the other part of the net so it would not slip and felt Charlie grab hold of it.

The plan was working.

Then Bishop heard a strange male voice – and felt his blood run cold.

"Well, well, well, look what we have here. It's one of the Magpies' football superstars."

The voice was not friendly. Emma was in trouble.

23. THE COMEBACK KID

Peter Bell raced into the Hall Park stadium with his dad trailing behind.

The cops had been great with him.

Once his dad had arrived, they raced through the questions about the kidnapping as fast as they could.

Peter had told them exactly what had happened, and nothing more.

Then they let him go – and gave him a chance to make the big game.

He flung his kit bag and coat into the away changing room without giving the messy room a second glance.

Then he darted up the tunnel as his dad wished him good luck from far behind.

The noise hit him first. He stood for a second and looked around. Packed to the rafters, the full stadium was an incredible sight.

Straight away, he saw the match had been stopped. Several medics were clustered around one of the goals with someone in agony on the floor.

Joe.

Peter grinned. Nice one buddy, he thought, as his eyes swept the rest of the pitch. The plan was obviously in full swing.

Something else was different. Magpies were wearing a ghastly orange kit while Peter was still in the usual green top.

Another time-wasting ploy. Brilliant.

"Peter, you made it! Well done. Are you okay?"

Barney approached him and threw a bright orange top in Peter's direction.

Peter did not question the change of strip. He spoke to the Magpies manager as he began to change on the touchline.

"I'm fine, boss. How long have we played for?"

"Two minutes."

Peter looked at the clock. It was 2.18pm. The time-wasting was working perfectly. Now he could help them out.

He looked at Barney, who gave a small wink.

Peter took a deep breath. This was it.

Charlie could still make the game. In fact, the way the game was going, they might still be playing tomorrow.

Barney called over Ted and told him to attract the referee's attention. He then turned back to Peter, who was tucking the shirt into his shorts.

"Right, Belly lad. You're playing on the left wing. Without Charlie and Emma, it is only Flem up front so mainly you'll be defending."

He placed a hand on Peter's shoulder and pointed towards the tall wiry lad on Rovers' right wing: Craig Handsom.

"This kid is a good player. He is quick and

dangerous but he doesn't like being tackled. And he definitely doesn't like getting muddy. Get stuck into him, lad."

Peter nodded.

The ref, a grey-haired man with a kind smile, ran to the touchline after spotting Ted's frantic waving.

Barney spoke quickly. "One of our players has arrived, ref. Can we put him on please?"

The Magpies boss pushed Peter on to the pitch without waiting for an answer.

"Wait."

Peter shivered. Only Chell Di Santos could manage to do that with a single word.

"This is not right. Is this some kind of trick? Surely both managers need to be consulted?"

Nervously, Peter glanced at the ref.

Barney spoke first.

"I must apologise, Chell. I spoke to the referee earlier but I could not find you before kick-off.

"There was an accident earlier in the day and some of our team have been delayed. That's why we started with only nine players."

Barney kept a straight face and looked directly at the opposition manager. The Demon Football Manager did not move a muscle in response.

Barney continued: "I know you're a champion of fair play so I assured the ref you would have no problem if the players caught up in the accident joined us a little late."

The referee added: "Yes, it is highly unusual but I had no problem with it once I heard both managers were happy. It's very sporting of you, Mr Di Santos. I am happy to allow this young fellow," – he pointed in Peter's direction – "and one more to enter the field of play and bring their team up to 11 players, whenever they arrive."

The ref smiled, unware of the simmering tension between the managers.

Di Santos offered the smallest nod of the head to indicate he would not protest further.

What else could he do? Barney had backed him into a corner.

Barney smiled. "Excellent. Glad that's sorted.

"Peter, over here, is first back. And we're expecting Toby and Charlie at any moment. They're fine – and we will be up to full strength in no time."

Barney's false smile never wavered. The managers locked eyes. Peter thought Chell Di Santos might explode.

Nobody moved. Then the Rovers manager turned and stomped back to his own bench.

The ref looked at Peter: "Right son, you're on. Wait here for my signal. As soon as the goalkeeper is fit to resume, you can come on. Understand?"

The winger nodded.

Joe was slowly getting to his feet in the far goalmouth. Peter never knew his friend was such a good actor.

Barney stood next to him.

"Mr Foster is doing a great job. Now it's your turn, Peter. Do whatever it takes to hold this game up. We must give them time to break the boys out."

Peter looked up: "But it is a lot to ask Bish and Emma to break them out. It is kids versus grown men over there."

Barney winked: "True … and that's why I have decided to even things up a little. They won't be alone for long."

24. THE OLD ENEMY

Adam Knight stood in front of Emma.

The sun glistened off his freshly shaven head.

His voice had its usual gloating tone.

Emma's hands curled into fists: "Why aren't you at the match?"

He shrugged. "I am still a Colts player – officially – so I am supposed to be at their match today.

"But I'm about to become Chell's captain and the new star striker at Rovers so why should I care about my old team?

"So I thought I would check out my new team Hall Park Rovers instead. A bit late, but I thought it would be fairly easy to nip across town with everyone being at Hall Park.

"But I was wrong, wasn't I? Because for some reason I can't understand, a gimp like you is lurking around here too."

The bully paused before his eyes narrowed.

"Now, if I remember correctly, didn't you knee me in the goolies a week ago?"

Emma swallowed. It was true.

She had lashed out at him when Magpies had played Colts.

She'd been sent off for it though and had regretted it ever since. It was the reason she was suspended for today's big game.

"Yes, I did … and you deserved it."

Adam smiled wickedly. "Fair enough. I'll just get my payback now instead."

Emma's mind raced. This idiot was going to ruin everything. If he looked up and saw Bishop and Charlie on the roof, it was over.

She dare not look upwards and give the game away. She prayed the boys would keep quiet too.

Emma put her hands out in front of her and took a step backwards. And then another.

"Look, it was a mistake, okay? I am sorry. I never should have done it."

Adam gazed at her and then made his move. He was quick, covering the ground between them in a couple of bounds.

He brushed Emma's hands aside with ease and grabbed a handful of her ponytail.

Emma wailed as he yanked her head towards him.

"Revenge is sweet, isn't it little Magpie girl?"

Emma didn't answer.

She couldn't – all the air unexpectedly rushed out of her body as both she and Adam collapsed on to the floor.

She groaned but realised the thug had lost his grip on her hair.

Someone else was with them on the floor too.

Bishop. The big striker had jumped from the roof and landed on top of Adam.

Bishop had crashed between the pair of them and it had allowed Emma to break free from the bully's grip.

Adam, on the other hand, was seeing stars.

Bishop crawled on top of him. He was strong enough to know Adam Knight would never be able to shift him – even in a mad rage.

Eyes filled with fury, Adam kicked wildly as he fought to remove the bigger boy off his chest.

It was no use. Bishop merely smiled back.

He did not move. He did not need to. His weight did the rest.

Emma could see Adam's face getting redder as he kicked hopelessly at his rival. She could see the air leaving him as Bishop's weight slowly crushed him.

Adam never knew when he was beaten. "Get off me, you loser. I've taken your place in the Rovers team because I'm the better player.

"The only way you can beat me is by being a coward and attacking me when my back is turned."

Emma wondered how Bishop would react.

She had fallen for Adam's dirty tricks last week. Would Bishop make the same mistake?

The sound of laughter told her the answer.

Bishop chuckled: "Adam, Adam, Adam. You are a better player than me – and probably less of a coward too.

"But I would rather be sitting where I am than you at the moment. Now you keep quiet, while we sort this whole mess out."

Bishop turned and looked up to the roof.

"Charlie?"

Charlie's head popped over the edge of the roof. He looked down at the scene and his eyes opened with surprise.

"Hi Em! What's up, Bish?"

"YOU! I'M GONNA ..." Adam Knight's eyes bulged as he saw the Boy Wonder.

Emma dropped to her knees and clamped a hand over Adam's mouth.

Bishop spoke quickly.

"Charlie, grab the net. We need to tie this dipstick up to stop him causing any more trouble."

Charlie hesitated.

"Bish, how are we going to get Toby out? Without the net and you down there, I can't reach him."

Emma replied. "We'll get Tobes out in a minute, Boy Wonder, I promise! Let's sort this problem out first though, eh?"

Charlie knew she was right. He scrambled up the roof and began to haul the goal net up.

He hissed into the room: "Don't worry, Toby. We're coming for you! We won't leave without you, I promise!"

The Boy Wonder did not wait for a reply. He lugged the net on to the roof and – with an almighty heave – chucked it over the side of the building.

Within moments, Emma was busy wrapping Adam Knight in a tangle of knots that the bully could never escape from.

By the time Charlie had landed safely on the ground next to them, Bishop was able to prise himself away from Adam, knowing he would not be able to escape.

"Thank you both."

Bishop waved a hand. "No problem. Now, how do we save Toby?"

None of them had an answer.

Emma spoke first: "You have to get to the game, Charlie. You go and we'll rescue Toby."

"No way. I'm not leaving him."

Charlie was not messing about.

Leaving without his friend was not an option.

"HEEEEELLLLLLLPPPPPP!"

Charlie, Bishop and Emma span round in horror.

They had stopped the bully from being able to move but his voice had done the damage.

Adam's eyes were shining with malice.

"HE IS GETTING AWAY ..."

Bishop clamped his hand over Adam's mouth but it was too late.

His shouting was loud enough for anyone nearby to hear.

Rexy would be coming.

25. DISASTER

It took three minutes for Peter to get warned about fouling by the referee.

A minute later he had a yellow card.

Craig Handsom, the Rovers' tricky winger, had been the danger man for the home side.

Barney had told Peter to mark him closely – and Peter did exactly that.

All of the time-wasting had turned the game into a scrappy match with hardly any goalmouth action.

Handsom had been the game's standout player so far.

He did not know Charlie or Toby so had no clue about the plans to halt the game.

To him and most of the Rovers team, this was the game of the season and they wanted to win.

They had no idea about the dirty tricks going on in the background. To them, it was merely a football game.

Peter did not complain about the booking. He knew it was deserved.

Handsom had floated past Flem without a second glance and was moving towards the Magpies penalty area before Peter stopped him in his tracks.

The slide tackle was perfectly timed – but was nowhere near the ball.

Handsom yelped as Peter ploughed through his legs as he prepared to shoot.

The ref blew: "Yellow card! Not the sort of behaviour we expect on the football pitch. If we see any more of it, you'll be having an early bath. Do you understand, Mr Bell?"

Peter nodded and did not argue with the punishment. There was no point trying to get out of this one.

Handsom did not complain either. He gave himself a quick dust down, checked his hair and headed into the penalty area without complaint.

Wrecka organised the Magpies defence as Rovers' central midfielder Dougie Fresh stepped up to take the free kick.

Fresh was the team's playmaker and everything went through him. Di Santos had snapped him up midway through the season from Wootton.

Joe had warned them about Rovers' new line-up but Peter was still shocked – he barely recognised any of the Rovers team from those early days of the season.

Flem and Billy Savage made up the wall. The wall was missing a player. Normally Charlie would be there but today they would do without.

Peter knew they needed to waste more time.

He could not do it by fouling either – or he faced getting sent off. And that would not help anyone.

Finally they were ready.

Fresh threw two arms into the air and began his run-up.

Seamus, Handsom and the other Rovers centre-back, Dan Burton, saw the signal and charged towards the back post.

It was a clever move. Half the Magpies team went with them, making other side of the goal less crowded.

Fresh struck the free-kick sweetly. But it did not go in the direction that everyone had been expecting.

Ignoring the runners, the Rovers midfielder hammered the ball past the two-man wall – exactly where Charlie should have been standing.

It went like a rocket and arrowed straight towards the bottom corner of the goal.

Mudder's view was blocked by the wall so he only saw the shot at the last moment.

The Magpies keeper threw himself to his left in a desperate attempt to keep it out.

The home fans began to rise in celebration. Peter waited for the net to ripple and the deafening roar that follows a goal.

Yet somehow Mudder reached it.

In a season of remarkable saves, this was easily his best. The end of his fingertips clipped the ball, and changed its path.

He could not stop the powerful shot but it was enough. Just.

The ball diverted on to the post and then trickled behind the goal for a corner kick.

Brave Mudder – once again the Magpies hero – ended up in a tangled heap in the goal's side-netting.

As the crowd behind the goal groaned with disbelief over the near miss, Peter bounced over to the hero goalkeeper.

"Good lad, Mudder. Now stay down, we can use up even more time here."

Mudder did not look up. The noise from the crowd was unreal – they could barely hear each other on the pitch.

Peter crouched down next to him. Then he realised: Mudder was crying.

"Darren, what's wrong?"

"My arm. I felt a snap. I think it's broken."

Peter jumped to his feet and began signalling to Ted to come on.

In the background he could see Di Santos and Barney begin to argue over yet another delay but he did not care.

He looked down at Mudder, whose face had turned a deathly white.

"Hurry!"

Peter knelt down and put an arm around his friend.

"You did it, Mudder. You saved it, like you always do. Hang in there, mate."

Mudder muttered something but Peter struggled to hear his words. He knelt down further.

"You need to win this ... for Charlie."

Peter gripped his friend's arm tightly. Ted was nearly halfway across the pitch. Help was almost here.

26. CAUGHT

Rexy tensed.

"HEEELLLPPPPPP!"

The scream had come from near the back of the clubhouse.

"Mambo, check the boys."

The goon did not need to be asked twice.

He leapt out of his seat and hurriedly began to untie the rope around the office door.

Rexy marched to the front door and peeked out of the window.

It was clear.

Seconds later Mambo was back.

"They're gone, boss!"

"What?"

"The little twerps are not in there! The window in the roof is open. I reckon they've done a bunk!"

Rexy did not believe him.

He ran to the small office to check for himself but Mambo was right: the boys had somehow managed to sneak out.

Another yell erupted nearby.

This time he could not make out the words.

His mind began to whirl. Mambo kept gibbering but Rexy ignored him.

He cursed himself for not protecting that window. How could he have been so careless? He had thought it was too high and small for the boys to escape.

Obviously he had been wrong.

Suddenly it clicked.

The scream: one of those idiots must have hurt themselves when they had jumped off the roof.

But they wouldn't be able to get far, particularly if one was injured.

Rexy looked at Mambo.

"Quick, you go round the left side of the building. I'll take the right side. We'll stop their escape one way or another."

Rexy turned and ran full pelt at the door. Mambo followed a few paces behind.

Rexy knew his future was on the line. Di Santos would refuse to pay if he did not meet his end of the deal.

The golden sand. The sparkling blue sea. The cocktails. The setting sun.

It was so close. Now his dream was in danger by two snotty-nosed kids who thought they were footballing superstars.

He could not let them get away.

Rexy hit the door at top speed.

His hands smashed into the door handle and sent it flying open.

He took one step out on the wooden decking and turned back to check Mambo was following.

BANG!

Before he could speak, the heavy wooden door flew straight back at him. The door thudded into the back of Rexy's head and sent him sprawling on the floor.

He groaned, unsure of what had happened.

His eyes found focus again.

A huge figure stood in the doorway.

It was that footballer guy Johnny Cooper. And he looked mad.

Rexy closed his eyes and groaned.

His head throbbed where the door had cannoned into him.

Coops had been standing behind the door and kicked it as Rexy had tried to leave.

When Coops spoke, Rexy could hear the anger bubbling inside him.

"Sit down. Shut up. The police are on their way. You two have had it. Now ... where are the boys?"

Rexy snorted.

Usually he would not have been scared of someone like Cooper but the blow from the door had left him seeing stars.

He knew he would not be able to stand up, let alone fight someone.

Coops stepped fully into the room. Mambo was pushed to the floor alongside Rexy. He did not protest.

Coops could not hide how furious he was.

"Well? Where have you and Di Santos hidden them?"

"We're here, Coops."

Surprised to hear a voice behind him, Coops twirled around to the open door.

Rexy peered around Cooper's big frame.

Charlie was standing there with a blonde girl behind him. He recognised her – she had been with them earlier in the newsagents.

How did she know where they'd taken them?

Rexy knew then it was over. There was no getting out of this one.

"Charlie! Thank goodness you are safe!" Coops grabbed the Boy Wonder in a bear hug.

"Well done, Emma! Where's Bishop and Toby?"

A voice piped up from Barney's office. Toby's face poked out from the doorway. His brown hair looked grey because of the dust.

He grinned: "I'm here, Coops. I was hiding in the office underneath the desk. They were in such a panic they didn't even realise I was still in there."

Coops marched over to Toby and hugged him too.

Rexy groaned. How could they have been so stupid? One of the boys had never even left the room!

Another voice came from outside the clubhouse.

"I'm here too, Coops ... I'm just keeping an eye on this rascal."

Coops let out a small chuckle.

"Good work, Bish. Well, well, well, if it is not Adam Knight. We seem to have got all Chell Di Santos's henchmen in one place."

Rexy watched a large ginger boy drag another lad into the room and plonked him down next to the door.

He was wrapped in an old goal net, meaning he could not move a muscle. His eyes were blazing with anger.

Rexy knew how he felt.

Charlie piped up: "To be fair, I don't think Adam

is part of this particular scheme."

Coops raised his eyebrows. "No?"

Bishop agreed. "Nah, it was simply a case of wrong place, wrong time for him.

"He would, of course, have happily stopped Charlie and Toby escaping but it didn't work out like that."

The gang laughed before Coops began to issue instructions.

"Okay. This is really simple.

"Emma, your dad is in the car park. He will take you, Charlie and Toby to Hall Park. With a bit of luck, you will make some of the game.

"Bish, I need you to stay here with me to keep an eye on this lot. The police are on their way so it shouldn't take too long."

He flicked his head towards Rexy and Mambo.

"What about him?" Toby nodded towards Adam.

Coops ran a hand through his hair as he weighed up the decision.

"Once you lot have disappeared, we'll let him go. For once, he hasn't done anything wrong."

For a second there was silence before Coops spoke again.

"What are you lot still doing here?

"There's a football match to be won at Hall Park – get out of here!"

Charlie paused and looked at Bishop and Coops. "Thank you."

Rexy watched the three kids turn and run out of the door.

His big money-making plan was finished.

And the police sirens could be heard in the distance.

27. NIGHTMARE

"Jimmy. You go in goal."

Ted barked out the order as he left the pitch.

Jimmy Welford was Magpies' reserve team goalkeeper. He had been playing on the right wing today with so many players missing.

However Mudder could not play on.

His wonder save had come at a price.

Ted did not think his arm was broken but wanted to send him to hospital on the edge of Crickledon for an X-ray to be sure.

Mudder's match – and season – was over.

It was a sad end for one of the players who had contributed so much to Magpies' unexpected success story.

The crowd warmly clapped as the goalkeeper walked slowly around the side of the pitch. His face remained pale as Ted guided him towards the changing room.

Peter clapped Jimmy on the back.

"Come on, Jimmy. You can do it."

Jimmy smiled as he pulled on his black and green gloves. Peter was not worried about him.

With his pink boots and shoulder-length blonde hair, Jimmy always stood out from the crowd. Nothing ever seemed to rattle him.

Peter did his best to hide the concern in his stomach.

With Mudder's unexpected departure, they were back to nine players – and Rovers had slowly taken control of the game.

He looked at the clock.

Only 25 minutes had been played.

But it was not enough.

They needed help – or the dream was over.

Handsom was standing over the corner kick waiting with his hands on hips. The ref blew to get the game restarted – yet again.

The corner was a wicked dipper. It was hit with real pace and fearsome dip.

Peter watched as it rocketed over the gaggle of players at the near post.

Sensibly, Jimmy didn't try to catch the ball. It was travelling too fast.

He stayed on his line, alongside Peter, as the ball dipped to the back post.

And Fresh was there to meet it with a sweetly timed, side-foot volley.

GOAL!

Jimmy and Peter looked at each other as the home crowd celebrated.

Neither of them had moved.

They did not have a chance against such an attack.

The Rovers players celebrated wildly near the corner flag with Fresh underneath the pile of bodies.

Chell Di Santos was on the pitch with his fists clenched in the direction of the Magpies bench.

Only Joe and Seamus did not celebrate for Rovers. Both stood still in their positions, waiting for the kick-off.

Di Santos spotted his captain and goalkeeper standing in their own half and signalled for them to join the rest of the team.

But they were not interested.

Peter could not help but smile as he watched the two Rovers players turn their backs on the Demon Football Manager.

Neither went near the huddle at the other end of the pitch.

He watched Di Santos try to keep his cool. The iceman was struggling to keep calm. Finally he gave up and stomped back to the bench.

As the Rovers began to untangle themselves and make their way back for the restart, Peter looked round at Magpies.

They looked shattered. No-one spoke a word. Several were looking at the floor.

They had given everything and it wasn't even half-time.

They had lost their goalkeeper. Emma was suspended. Their star player still wasn't here. And they only had nine players.

Belly clapped his hands.

"COME ON, MAGPIES. THIS LOT ARE RUBBISH."

Wrecka responded immediately.

"Peter's right. Come on, Magpies, we're not beaten yet!"

One by one, the Magpies players began clapping

and shouting. They still believed.

But they weren't the only ones.

A roar from the crowd stole Peter's attention.

It started from the main stand and swept around the stadium until it was nearly deafening.

Peter was confused. What now?

And then he saw what the fuss was about.

Charlie had appeared on the touchline along with Toby. They were both talking to Barney and the referee.

His heart leapt.

Bishop and Emma had done the impossible.

The boys had made it.

Magpies were back in business.

28. COWARD

Chell Di Santos could not believe his eyes.

Everything had been going so well.

Despite the obvious time-wasting and the play-acting, his wonderful team had risen above the nonsense and had taken a thoroughly deserved lead.

The title was nearly his.

The big job offers would soon follow, he knew.

But Rexy had failed.

Charlie Fry was standing 10 metres away from him.

How could this have happened?

He checked his phone.

No word from Rexy.

Magpies were now planning to bring rat-boy Fry and his little pal into the game.

Di Santos knew this could change everything.

The so-called Football Boy Wonder had already ruined too much this season. He would not let it happen again.

He marched over to the huddle with the two boys, Barney and the referee.

Barney was busy talking: "... you two get your shirts on and we'll be bringing them on the next time the ball goes out of play. Are you happy with that arrangement, ref?"

The ref did not get an opportunity to reply as Di Santos steamed into the conversation.

"No! This cannot happen. It is against the rules! I would rather forfeit the game than have changes every two seconds.

"I've already let one player join the game late. Now we have two more who couldn't be bothered to turn up on time.

"This is not merely a kickabout at a park – this is a proper game. I will not allow this type of nonsense to happen."

Di Santos tried to keep his voice calm as the words flooded out. He could not worry about how Charlie Fry had escaped his trap. He needed to focus.

Di Santos looked at the ref for an answer. The match official scratched his head as he tried to work out what should be done.

The Rovers boss allowed himself the smallest of smiles. He had won. He was too quick for the likes of the dimwit ref and that idiot Barney.

Charlie Fry would not be playing in today's game. He was sure of it.

Barney threw a couple of spare orange shirts to the boys standing nearby.

"Like I said, pull your shirts on and warm up. We'll kick the ball straight out of play and you will both be on in a minute."

Di Santos could not believe his ears.

"What? They will not!"

Barney turned back to Di Santos.

"We have enough players so the game cannot be forfeited on our part. Is that correct, ref?"

The ref nodded.

"Excellent. Now, we used one sub earlier when Belly came on. Now I wish to use two more. My final two subs."

The ref shrugged: "In 20 years of being a referee, I have never come across this situation. However Mr Payne's proposal is sensible. I do not have a problem with it."

Di Santos could feel the heat rising in his neck.

"No! I will not allow it."

Barney moved closer and made Di Santos take half a step backwards.

He hissed quietly so the ref could not hear: "You will – or everyone in this ground will soon know why half my team is missing."

Di Santos felt as if he had been punched in the stomach.

His anger turned to panic. His mind raced with a heap of questions.

Surely they didn't know? Or did they?

Had Rexy betrayed him? Were the police coming?

Barney did not wait for an answer. He spoke loudly so the ref could hear again.

"Excellent. We have an agreement. I'll tell the boys."

Speechless, Di Santos watched the Magpies manager and the ref move away.

He had been outfoxed.

But the game – and the league – was not over yet.

29. COMEBACK

Charlie took a deep breath as a wave of nerves and excitement came over him.

Toby muttered something but he could not hear due to the noise.

The atmosphere was electric: 10,000 people packed into a stadium for a junior football match.

Charlie looked around at the sea of faces.

He was desperate to get out there and play. It was the biggest game of his life and he was only here because of the efforts of his amazing friends.

As the ball rolled out for a throw in, the ref indicated for them to come on. Toby raced towards the Magpies goal to take his usual slot at left-back.

Gary Bradshaw would push into left midfield and allow Peter to join Charlie up front. Flem would switch to the right wing.

Charlie knelt down and rubbed the immaculate turf.

He was back at Hall Park. And he had a point to prove.

"Come on Charlie! Come on Charlie!"

The Magpies fans were singing his name.

Goosebumps appeared again. He could do it.

With a sprint, he entered the pitch as the noise from the packed crowd went up another level.

He trotted in the direction of Joe's goal. The opposition goalkeeper gave him a huge smile and thumbs up.

Charlie couldn't believe they had not even reached half-time. They should have been deep into the second half by now.

He knew his friend – despite playing on the opposite side – had something to do with it.

But now the game was on.

Joe played for Rovers, Charlie played for Magpies.

Charlie knew exactly how much his friend wanted to win.

The Boy Wonder took a deep breath. It was game time.

"Welcome back, Fry-inho."

Seamus stood close behind him.

"Glad you made it. Foster told me about the problems this morning. Bang out of order."

Charlie smiled at Seamus. Instantly he knew the Rovers captain had helped too.

"Thanks," he replied.

"No problem, just don't score against us!" Seamus slapped him on the back.

Charlie grinned.

Annie had the ball. Charlie knew where the ball was going before she made the pass.

It flew straight over their heads.

Charlie's deeper position had forced Seamus to move higher up the pitch, leaving a gap in the Rovers back line.

Peter was on to it in a flash.

He waited for the ball to drop over his shoulder

and then hit it goalwards without even looking.

The ball fizzed and dipped towards the Rovers goal. Joe, however, was positioned perfectly.

He threw himself backwards and arched his back to reach the ball. A gloved hand pushed the ball over the bar.

"OOOOHHHHH!"

At last the Magpies fans had something to cheer.

Even though it was Rovers' home game, Charlie guessed half the crowd were on their feet cheering Peter's effort.

Joe began to bark orders to the defenders in front of him. He gave Peter a crafty wink as he ran over to take the corner.

Charlie grinned to himself. Peter would be so mad.

The corner came in but was easily headed out by Seamus.

It flew out of the penalty area high above most of the players.

The ball landed at the feet of Handsom, who turned in the blink of an eye and began to race towards the near-empty Magpies half.

"AARRRGGGHHHH!"

Annie appeared from nowhere. Her slide tackle took the ball and Handsom off the pitch.

"Great tackle!" The crowd applauded as Annie dusted herself down and offered Handsom a helping hand to get back to his feet.

The winger accepted and patted down his trendy hairstyle as he rejoined the pitch.

The throw-in was intercepted by Toby, who nipped in ahead of Rovers full-back Sam Knowl.

He looked for Charlie and a clever pass found the Boy Wonder in a couple of metres of space.

It was the opportunity Charlie wanted.

He knew Seamus would have to close him down but Peter and Greavesy were already racing ahead.

The movement made Seamus unsure whether to close Charlie down or help pick up the attacking runners.

Joe screamed for him to close the ball down but Seamus still hesitated.

And that was exactly what Charlie needed. He drove deep into the Rovers half in the centre of the pitch.

Peter and Greavesy both pulled left, taking defenders with them. Seamus finally decided to tackle Charlie but it was too late.

"Now, Charlie!"

Flem had galloped up the right wing unseen and completely unmarked. With a flick of his eye, the magic target locked on the edge of the penalty area.

It flashed green and Charlie pulled the trigger: dropping a beautiful reverse pass straight into Flem's path.

Joe read the situation and raced out of his goal.

Flem managed to beat the keeper to the ball – but only just. The Magpies player got a toe to the ball before the keeper was upon him.

The ball looped up and dropped a fraction wide of the post, leading to groans of disbelief from Magpies players and fans. Close, but not enough.

The half-time whistle blew.

Magpies had 45 minutes to score twice and win the championship that no-one gave them a hope of winning at the start of the season.

30. CHAMPIONS

Barney stood in the centre of the changing room.

The Magpies players were tired and thirsty after a half where they had spent most of the game with only nine players.

It suited Barney. He had something important to tell the team and he didn't want to be interrupted.

"Lads ... and lasses.

"You have done me proud today. Not just on the pitch but in the bizarre events leading up to the game too."

Some of the boys looked confused. Barney ignored them. There was no time to explain.

"These last seven to eight months have been like a dream for me. You are the best team I have ever managed without a doubt."

Several eyes flicked towards Charlie. Barney spotted it straight away.

"Not just Charlie. Or Annie. Or Wrecka. It is all of you.

"As a team, I have never known anything like it. You are an incredible bunch and you have done me proud ever since we started this adventure.

"Win, lose or draw, you will always be champions

in my eyes."

He paused for a moment.

"I know you're tired. I know a lot has happened today. I know they are a good team.

"But this is our chance. Let's win it for Emma. Let's win it for Mudder. Let's win it for ourselves."

The Magpies dressing room erupted, the tiredness forgotten. Within seconds they were bouncing on to the pitch ready for the second half.

Charlie walked out with Annie behind the rest.

"You can do it, Charlie Fry."

He looked at his friend: she was always so positive; so determined; so certain of herself.

"Thanks ... Annie Cooper. I'll try, I promise."

She ruffled his hair and ran off.

Charlie tried to concentrate and block out the crowd. Two goals in one half of football. He could do it, couldn't he?

There was one serious obstacle: Joe.

Magpies started the second half like they ended the first: relentlessly attacking the Rovers goal.

But Joe was everywhere.

He pushed a thumping header from Wrecka over the bar, smothered a sneaky snapshot from Billy Savage and denied Peter again in a one-on-one.

Charlie could not get into the game. The ball, it seemed, was always on the opposite side of the pitch to him.

He tried to keep calm but time was running out.

With ten minutes left, the Boy Wonder began to panic. He had barely touched the ball in the second half.

Magpies were camped into the Rovers half. A counter-attack goal would finish their title hopes but they had no choice.

A draw meant Rovers would win the title: it was win or bust for Magpies.

Joe's legs stopped a rasping drive from Greavesy and gave Peter the opportunity to send in yet another corner kick.

This time though Seamus got the clearance wrong.

He marked Wrecka, expecting a near-post flick-on, and could only watch with horror as the ball sailed over their heads to the back post.

One player waiting: Annie.

She met the ball firmly, heading the ball down into the corner.

Joe reached the ball at the last second but could only push it towards the post.

It hit the inside of the woodwork, rolled along the line and dribbled into the goal a second before Fresh could whack it clear.

GOAL!

Half the stadium, the bench and the Magpies players screamed with delight and looked to the ref.

He paused for a second as he slowly reached for his whistle.

A quick blast and a point to the centre circle indicated a goal. The stadium erupted again.

YEEESSSSSSS!

1-1.   Seven minutes left.

The next goal would decide the Crickledon Under-13s championship.

Straight from kick-off, Toby won the ball and Magpies were back on the attack.

Wrecka urged the team forward. Rovers had everyone back apart from Handsom, who was lingering on the halfway line.

Annie and Wrecka watched the Rovers striker while the rest of the team poured forward in search of the goal that would win the title.

But Handsom was clever. He moved towards Annie one moment, Wrecka the next.

The constant movement caused confusion. Both Annie and Wrecka thought the other one was marking Handsom – but, in fact, neither did.

Still it did not matter.

Handsom might be a danger but Rovers could not get hold of the ball.

Time ticked down. There were two minutes left.

Peter danced around Fresh before being chopped down by several Rovers players trying to rob the ball away from him.

The ref blew immediately and pointed for a Magpies free-kick. Charlie's stomach flipped a couple of times.

His chance had arrived.

The free-kick was in his territory: in the centre of the goal and a couple of metres outside the Rovers penalty area.

It was far enough out to get the ball over the wall and down again into the goal but close enough to still put real power on the shot.

Charlie placed the ball.

Joe would expect him to clip the ball over the wall. With the target, he had practiced that shot every day for months.

So Charlie would call his bluff. The wall lined up to Charlie's right – covering the left side of the goal.

Joe stood on his tiptoes a metre away from the right-hand post.

The whistle went.

With the blink of an eye, Charlie locked the target above Joe's head and booted the ball with every single ounce of strength he had.

He knew Joe would move and the ball would sail straight into the place he currently stood.

Charlie fell as the ball soared towards the goal.

As he crashed down to the floor, he watched the ball fizz past the Rovers wall – exactly where he'd placed the target.

One small problem though.

Joe hadn't moved like Charlie thought he would do.

The ball went straight to him.

With a big jump, his large hands stopped the shot in mid-flight and pushed it down to the ground with ease.

Charlie shook his head. Joe had outfoxed him.

A groan of disappointment came from the crowd at the near miss.

But the danger wasn't over.

Joe had scooped the ball up and launched it down the pitch.

Handsom was waiting. Annie knew straight away she was in trouble. She had thought Wrecka was marking him – but Wrecka was even further away from the Rovers winger than she was.

In desperation, she looked around for any other defenders. Of course, there was no-one else around.

Everyone else was up the pitch. Handsom was clean through with only Jimmy to beat.

Jimmy raced out to narrow the angle but Handsom blasted past the Magpies keeper like he wasn't even there.

He put his hands up to celebrate the league-winning goal as he evaded Jimmy's lunge.

Chell Di Santos was on the pitch.

So were the Rovers subs.

But they had underestimated Jimmy Welford.

The reserve keeper flung himself full-length as Handsom prepared to roll the ball in the net. He could not stop the shot but his fingertips brushed the ball.

It was all that was needed.

The ball changed direction and clattered into the post. Jimmy's dive sent Handsom flying to the floor so he could not tap the ball home.

Instead it was an exhausted Annie who pounced on the ball and thumped it back up the field.

Magpies' title dreams were somehow still alive – for another minute at least.

31. FINAL SCORE

"UP! GET UP THE PITCH, MAGPIES!"

Barney roared at his team as Annie booted the ball clear.

Everything seemed to be happening in slow motion.

Chell Di Santos was screaming instructions too.

The ball sailed high. It cleared the managers and the subs that should not have been on the pitch in the first place.

It shot past the midfielders and finally landed a couple of metres ahead of Seamus and Peter, who were wrestling each other.

The recent warm weather had made the pitch turn rock hard.

So the high bounce surprised everyone – going straight over Peter and Seamus. As he realised the fresh danger, Joe raced off his line to claim the ball.

But Annie's clearance had begun to run out of gas. The bounce was high but also slow and loopy. It wouldn't carry to Joe.

Out of nowhere, a Magpies player ran past Seamus.

Toby.

He brought the ball neatly under control and looked up to see Joe bearing down on him.

Toby did not panic.

He watched the Rovers goalkeeper get closer and prepared to chip the ball into the empty net behind him.

"OOOOMMMPPPPHHHHHHHHH!"

Toby crashed to the ground before he managed to get the shot away. The ball ran harmlessly through to Joe.

Seamus had barged into the back of Toby before he could shoot.

"PENALTY!"

The scream was deafening. Thousands of people appealed at the same time and every person turned to the referee.

His whistle blew immediately.

He pointed to the spot.

"YESSS!"

Charlie could feel everybody in the ground look at him.

He swallowed.

He felt exhausted.

So much had happened today: the kidnap; the great escape; the time-wasting plan; the end-to-end championship thriller.

He felt strange. It had been the oddest day he could remember.

Now, after everything that had happened, he was taking the most important penalty of his life against his oldest friend.

He picked the ball up and refused to look in Joe's direction. Best friends or not, he would not break his concentration for anyone.

He remembered his dad's advice: concentrate only on the ball and nothing else.

Charlie blanked out everything. People were talking to him, slapping him on the back, bumping into him.

He did not care. It did not matter.

The ball. Focus on the ball.

The ref's whistle blew.

Focus.

Charlie flicked his eyes to the top right-hand corner.

He knew Joe's weaker hand was his left one – and that was exactly where he planned to plant the penalty.

The target locked and flashed green.

It was time.

Charlie did not hesitate – he ran up and struck the ball with all of the power that he had left in his body.

It went like a rocket. It was headed exactly where he wanted it to go.

But then Charlie's eyes widened. Joe was diving the right way.

However he was underneath the ball, moving towards the bottom corner. The ball was going above him into the top corner.

Charlie had done it.

Magpies had won the league.

Then in slow motion, a large gloved hand rose up out of nowhere.

The ball crashed into Joe's palm.

Charlie felt as if time had slowed to a crawl. Joe could not catch the ball because it was above his diving lunge.

But was his effort enough to keep it out?

Joe's hand was strong. The ball cannoned off his glove and changed direction, away from Charlie's target.

It crashed into the crossbar ... and bounced away from the goal.

The Boy Wonder sank to his knees as the referee blew his whistle to bring the epic match to a close.

Magpies had lost the championship by a single kick.

32. THE FOOTBALL SUPERSTAR

"Champions! Champions! Champions!"

Charlie watched from a distance while Joe was thrown in the air by excited teammates as they lined up for the league presentation

The goalkeeper had been carried around the pitch after his last gasp penalty save had won the title for Rovers.

Charlie's own shattered teammates had rallied round, clapping him the back and ruffling his hair despite their own disappointment.

"We'll get them next year, Boy Wonder."

"So unlucky, Charlie."

"You know you're still the best player in England, don't you?"

The crowd had applauded Barney's outstanding team too.

They appreciated how far Magpies had come – from bottom of the league to within a whisker of winning the competition against all the odds.

Magpies had completed a downbeat lap of honour.

They had clinched promotion too but it was hard to celebrate after being so close to winning the title.

They kept well away from the celebrations at the

other end of the pitch after the usual handshakes had finished.

Now they huddled as group in the centre circle. Charlie stood away from the others on the edge of the penalty area.

Strangely, Charlie didn't feel terrible. He could not have done much more. Joe had simply been too good.

The Boy Wonder watched Seamus lead the Rovers team along the line up of important-looking people with the trophy at the end of the line.

Joe was the last player to take a medal followed by a grinning Chell Di Santos.

A silver-haired chap with glasses, who Charlie assumed was the club's president, stepped forward with the league trophy – a small silver cup with a dented lid – in his hands.

"Ladies and gentlemen. After a truly thrilling final, it gives me great honour to announce the winners of this year's Crickledon Under-13s League is ... Hall Park Rovers."

A loud cheer went up. Hardly any of the crowd had left even though the game finished 15 minutes ago.

Charlie watched as Seamus shook the chap's hand and took the trophy.

However Chell Di Santos was too fast.

He eased Seamus's hands from the cup and yanked it fully from the grip of the surprised chairman.

Charlie was certain the Rovers boss looked directly at him as he lifted the cup, screaming at the top of his voice.

Seamus, Joe and the other Rovers players lifted their hands in the air to celebrate their achievement.

A roar from the crowd greeted them in response.

A photographer for the Crickledon Telegraph was busy snapping away as the jubilant Rovers team lined up for the winning team photo.

Charlie watched Barney move among his team as he offered sympathy and encouragement to his players.

The Boy Wonder began to walk towards his friends. He wanted to thank Barney for everything had had done for him – he owed him that much.

A familiar voice stopped him in his tracks.

"You missed that on purpose, didn't you?"

Peter stood a couple of yards in front of him.

Belly had not spoken to Charlie since he had missed the penalty – and now Charlie knew exactly why.

"What?"

Eyes blazing, Peter could barely control his temper.

"You missed. Twice! The free-kick and then the penalty.

"I know your secret, Charlie Fry! You never, ever miss – unless you want to!

"What I want to know is: why?"

Peter's hands curled into fists. A tear of frustration trickled down his cheek.

Charlie took a deep breath.

"Oh ... Peter."

"What?"

Charlie knew he should have felt angry. He should have been upset. He should have felt devastated at missing the most important kick of his life.

But he didn't. In fact, he felt almost happy.

"Don't be mad.

"I wish I had scored, of course, but I promise I

didn't miss anything on purpose."

Charlie began to walk in Peter's direction.

"I gave everything to win that match – and it wasn't enough.

"The target placed the ball exactly where I wanted it to go and I hit both efforts with everything I had.

"Usually, that is enough ... but today it wasn't."

Charlie reached his friend and put an arm round Peter's shoulder. He pointed towards Joe.

"I threw everything at him but he was too good.

"I can't do any more than that, can I?"

The friends gazed together in Joe's direction again.

He was being interviewed by Andrew Hallmakr, the reporter from the Crickledon Telegraph, at the side of the pitch.

When Peter spoke again, his tone had changed. The anger had gone.

"Wait a minute, do you mean ..."

Charlie nodded before Peter had finished the sentence.

"That's right. He really is that good.

"Even with the magic target, he kept the ball out."

Charlie smiled and added: "I may be the Football Boy Wonder but Joe, it turns out, is the Football Superstar."

SIX WEEKS LATER

"Let me see!"

"No! Get off!"

Peter and Charlie battled for the tablet. They were the only two players still in the changing rooms.

It did not matter though.

They were guaranteed places for Hall Park Magpies next season. The trials had been arranged to try to find some exciting new talent to join the team.

And plenty of kids had turned out to show their skills.

But the boys had something more exciting on their minds.

It had started as a rumour but now the Crickledon Telegraph had confirmed it.

Peter kept hold of his tablet. A flick of a finger and the short story flashed up in front of them.

Championship-winning manager arrested

Detectives today arrested Hall Park's highly-rated youth manager Chell Di Santos.

In an early morning raid, police arrested the Italian-born manager in his home in connection with a kidnap case.

Police confirmed they had taken the 39-year-old into custody for questioning but refused to answer any further questions.

Di Santos masterminded Hall Park Rovers Under 13's recent title triumph and had been in talks with several league sides in the past few weeks.

Peter punched Charlie on the arm.

"Got him!"

Charlie shook his head in amazement.

"I can't believe it. I thought he'd got away with it!"

The gang had spent weeks wondering why Di Santos was able to march around Crickledon with a smug look on his face.

But the truth, it appeared, was beginning to catch up with him.

Charlie didn't know who was behind it. Perhaps Mambo. Or Rexy. Maybe Adam Knight spilled the beans on the Demon Football Manager.

In truth, he didn't care. Di Santos had been caught. Now he would have to pay the penalty.

Charlie bounced up: "Come on Belly. Let's put this lot through their paces. Think we'll find anyone who will suit us?"

Peter knew what Charlie meant. Magpies were not a normal team. It was not all about talent: it was about character too.

You could be the best player in the world but, if you did not work hard and be a team player, then you weren't right for Magpies.

Charlie opened the door with Peter a couple of steps behind him.

They stopped and looked at the scene in front of them: Manor Park was packed with wannabe footballers.

The pitch had been divided into three smaller areas – it gave kids the chance to show their skills with less room than usual.

Three people sat on old wooden chairs with a rickety bench in front of them. All were talking quietly and making notes.

Barney, Ted and Coops had their backs to Charlie and Peter but knew they had finally left the changing room: a ripple of excitement went round the pitches as the Boy Wonder emerged into full daylight.

"Ah Mr Fry and Mr Bell. Nice of you to join us." Barney spoke without looking.

Charlie shuffled uncomfortably. "Sorry boss, we were ... er..."

Barney waved to stop Charlie talking so Peter changed the subject.

"Looks busy, boss. Anyone caught your eye?"

Coops turned to face them. "Oh yeah, we've found handful of strikers that are awesome – far better than the ones we currently have got."

Charlie and Peter grinned. They knew Coops' sense of humour well enough now to only believe half the things he said.

Barney did not look at them but pointed towards the far match.

"That lad is a player. We'll be taking him."

Charlie squinted into the distance – and broke into a huge smile.

Bishop had been unsure whether to turn out for the trials or not. Thankfully they had managed to persuade him to do it.

It looked like he would be with them next season.

A fourth person plonked themselves on the bench alongside the older men: Joe.

"Any potential goalkeepers out there, Mr Foster?"
Ted asked.

Joe shrugged. "Perhaps, although we're pretty well
stocked with keepers with Jimmy and Mudder at the
moment."

He noticed Charlie and Peter and waved before
turning back to his pad.

Joe no longer played youth football at this level.

United had offered him a scholarship after his
heroics in the championship decider.

It meant he could no longer play down the park or
play for Magpies or Rovers. He could not risk getting
injured.

However United did allow Joe to help out with
coaching at Magpies – a role he was delighted to
accept.

Charlie was happy for his friend.

Joe's performances throughout the season had
been sensational and now he was part of one of the
biggest clubs in England. No-one deserved it more.

"Right you two grinning herberts, the match on
the right is short of two players. One on each team,
when you have finished your social club ..."

Barney was cut off in mid-sentence and he turned
to see who had interrupted him.

"I need one of those slots, mister."

A gangly lad with dark curly shoulder-length hair
stood behind them.

He was lazily playing keepy-uppy with a ragged old
football.

The tatty ball looked as if it was connected to his
foot with a piece of string.

"Who are you?" Peter asked the question for the
rest.

The lad chuckled. "I'm the greatest footballer you'll ever see."

Everyone turned to look at the boastful kid behind them.

"What's your name?"

Barney eyed the newcomer suspiciously.

The boy trapped the ball with a flourish.

"I'm Ad Leeshinski."

Leeshinski turned to Charlie.

"So the big boys didn't come knocking then, Boy Wonder?"

"Er …." Charlie did not know what to say.

The offers had come in – United, City, Rovers, the Reds – they were all desperate for him to sign.

But the offer he longed for had not arrived: the Blues had not been in contact.

And, as far as Charlie was concerned, Hall Park Magpies was the only other team he wanted to play for – apart from the Blues.

So he had stayed put.

"Yeah, I'll be here next season."

Leeshinski rubbed his chin.

"Man, we are going to be some team next season."

Coops appeared next to them. "Okay, let's see what you've got, kiddo. How do you spell your name?"

"Easy. Spell it how you say it: 'LEE-SHIN-SKI'. How anyone gets it wrong is beyond me."

With that he grabbed the bib in Coops' hands and trotted on to the field.

Coops shook his head at the boy's brashness.

"I'm having the other spot," Peter growled before he raced over to join the match that Leeshinski had entered moments earlier.

Charlie knew what was coming. Peter hated show-offs. It did not take long. On small pitches, everyone was involved for most of the game.

The ball seemed to be attracted to Leeshinski. He glided past people – his legs seemed to be extendable, which meant the ball was never out of his control.

Peter attempted to slide tackle him. A beautiful back heel sent him the wrong way.

Such outrageous skill only wound Peter up more. He twirled around and ran directly at Leeshinski, who had anticipated the response.

He calmly sidestepped the challenge before a nutmeg completed Peter's humiliation.

Without even looking at the goal, Leeshinski swerved Wrecka's sliding tackle and finished with a thunderbolt into the top corner, which left the keeper rooted to the spot.

Peter still looked hot and bothered when the short match ended a few minutes later.

Barney and the others had been busy scribbling notes as Leeshinski had turned on the magic.

Charlie chuckled. "He made you look pretty stupid, Belly."

"Well ... er ... he can play a bit. I'll give him that."

Leeshinski draped two arms around the boys' necks as they stopped for a breather.

He grinned: "I told you: I am the best. You may be the Football Boy Wonder but you've met your match now, Charlie Fry.

"Luckily for the both of you, we're going to be on the same side.

"We are going to be unbeatable. Believe."

ACKNOWLEDGMENTS

The Football Superstar may have been my
brainchild but it could not have been created without
the help of various people.
In no particular order, they are:
Richard Wayte proofread The Football Superstar
with meticulous precision. I find writing consistently
throws up new grammar puzzles and Richard remains
my first port of call at moments of indecision.
Overlap queen Alicia Babaee did a somewhat
belated edit but provided surprisingly sensible advice
when I needed it most.
Designer Mark Newnham for creating an
outstanding cover as usual. In return, I offered some
valuable clothing and fashion advice, which I know
was gratefully received.
Virgin Active in Collingtree for its outstanding
attitude to inclusion and helping people with a
disability. Having such a supportive gym enables me
to remain relatively healthy and out of the clutches of
hospital.
And lastly to my family and friends – who help me
in so many ways.
With almost two decades of writing experience
behind me, I can comfortably say that creating the
Charlie Fry Series is one of my biggest achievements.

But it is so much more than that.

Charlie's adventure has been embraced by so many children and has hopefully contributed in a small way to raising awareness about CF in the younger generations. It never fails to amaze me how children desperately want our Boy Wonder to succeed. It is an incredible feeling.

Thank you for being a part of it.

As I've said previously, this is the last part of the Charlie Fry story. However I plan to write a collection of shorter ebook stories, featuring Charlie and the gang in the future.

A taste of my next book – The Pumpkin Code – is over the page.

**

Martin Smith lives in Northamptonshire with his wife Natalie and daughter Emily.

He is a qualified journalist and, when he is not writing, he works part-time as a Social Media Manager.

He has cystic fibrosis, diagnosed with the condition as a two-year-old.

The Charlie Fry series is about friendship, self-belief and a love of football — the one sport that seems to unite people of all backgrounds under one cause.

COMING SOON

THE PUMPKIN CODE

Kids in fancy dress fill the streets.
Laughter echoes down the roads as sweet buckets
rattle in doorways.
It is Halloween.
It is the night of the Pumpkin Code.
But something awful is lurking in the shadows.
Evil waiting to pounce – and the dark October night
of Halloween provides the perfect opportunity.
Thirteen-year-old Artie Eason stumbles on the
terrible secret by mistake.
But can he save everyone who is trick-or-treating
before it is too late?
Beware the pumpkins.
Beware the code. Or else.

**The Pumpkin Code is the next story from Martin
Smith, author of the bestselling Charlie Fry
Series.
It is a Halloween scary story, aimed at young
people aged between 10 and 14.**

ALSO BY MARTIN SMITH

The Football Superstar is part five of the best-selling Charlie Fry Series.

All of Charlie's earlier adventures are listed below:

The Football Boy Wonder

The Demon Football Manager

The Magic Football Book

The Football Spy

The entire Charlie Fry Series is available via Amazon in print and on Kindle today.

Follow the series on:

Facebook
Facebook.com/footballboywonder

Instagram
@charliefrybooks

Martin Smith

The Football Superstar

Made in the USA
Coppell, TX
19 February 2021

50532122R00080

3 1170 01127 7377